MOUNT SNOW

A.C. HESSENAUER

For my boys. You know who you are.

Playlist

1. The Underdog- Spoon
2. Power Over Me- Dermot Kennedy
3. The Cave- Mumford & Sons
4. I Am Happy- AWOLNATION
5. White Flag- Bishop Briggs
6. You're Somebody Else- flora cash
7. WONDERLAND- NEONI
8. You're Gonna Go Far, Kid- The Offspring
9. Teenagers- My Chemical Romance
10. Hands Down- Dashboard Confessional
11. Sugar, We're Going Down- Fall Out Boy
12. Could Have Been Me- The Struts
13. Vindicated- Dashboard Confessional
14. Make It All Right- The Offspring
15. Kill Your Heroes- AWOLNATION
16. Welcome to the Black Parade- My Chemical Romance
17. Jeff The Killer (Piano Version) [Sweet Dreams Are Made of Screams]- Myuu

CONTENTS

"I must not fear. Fear is the mind-killer.
The little-death that brings total obliteration.
I will face my fear. I will permit it to pass over me and through me.
And when it has gone past, I will turn the inner eye to seek its path.
For where the fear has gone there will be nothing.
Only I will remain."

- Litany Against Fear,
Dune, by Frank Herbert

1

— . —

I held the steering wheel loosely in one hand, lost in thought as the miles ticked by. I estimated we still had ten miles to go before the next turn. *Right on Hiddleston, left onto Groesbeck.*

"What color?" Dad broke through my internal recitation. I instinctively lifted my right hand and placed it back on the steering wheel. *Ten and two.*

I cleared my throat, careful to keep my eyes level, on the road ahead. I could sense him watching me out of my periphery. "Black pickup," I replied, in a tone that I hoped would sound casual. But it came out as more of a question than an answer, my voice lifting up on that last syllable.

Dad turned to face forward again, nodding. My grip relaxed slightly, and I felt the corners of my mouth twitch. When I could sense he was no longer paying attention to me, I allowed my gaze to flick up to the rearview mirror.

There was the black pickup truck. It had dropped further back, maybe another dozen car lengths, but it was still there, the first car in the lane behind us. I let out a breath and held my hand out to him. That had been a lucky one. He glanced at my open palm for a second, then handed the MapQuest print-out to me wordlessly.

Paper rustled as I gripped it, sliding my thumb down, eyes shifting between scanning the paper and back up to the road.

"How much farther?" Dad asked, as he ran his hands through his short greying hair. He sighed and smoothed both hands over his eyebrows. Fingers pressing against his eyelids for a moment as he leaned forward. He dropped his hands and rotated his head, stretching his neck. Clearly, he had been sitting there tense and alert, even though I had been the one driving for the past two hours. I gritted my teeth and focused back on the print-out. He still didn't trust me. I had taken driver's ed almost two years ago, but I was still on my practice license.

I was shocked when he insisted I drive for the bulk of the trip to Vermont. He was always saying I needed to practice more, giving me tips and reminders, but he never seemed to want to climb into the passenger seat with me behind the wheel.

Mom had done a better job. She would ask me to take her on little trips to the post office or the grocery store. I always groaned when she did, but it was only half-hearted. She was calm when I drove; she didn't put me on edge.

I could feel Dad's anxiety seeping into me, making me doubt myself. I was a good driver. Good enough. It wasn't about me, anyway, I reminded myself. It said more about him—his need for control, than it did about my driving ability.

"Ah, let me see." I peered down again, adding up the miles in my head. "We're about seven miles away. Getting close now." *Right on Hiddleston, left onto Groesbeck.* I repeated the refrain several times in my head. I had been right.

Dad murmured something I didn't catch. I turned to him. "What?" I asked, letting the printout fall onto the center console between us. He stared straight ahead, but jerked his head back towards the rear of the car.

"You got lucky," he said, voice clipped. "The black pickup."

I clenched my jaw and turned back to focus on the road ahead. My hands at ten and two, gripping the steering wheel. So he *had* noticed. Great.

"You weren't sure." He looked at me and gave me a slight grin. "You were lucky." He patted my leg for a moment, two brief taps. "You're a good driver, Ted." I felt my eyebrows raise in surprise but quickly smoothed over my features again, replacing my mask of stoicism.

"But you can't just be good, you have to be great. Excellent." He looked back at the road, then back at me, eyeing me closely as if he didn't think I was listening, or hadn't heard him again. "You have to be constantly on alert. Hypervigilant. You need to drive defensively. Always expect the driver next to you to make the wrong move; a dangerous decision. Always be aware of your surroundings." I was listening, it was just that I'd heard it all before.

"I know, Dad," I said softly.

"You know?" He leaned away from me, brows raised.

"Dad, come on," I started, but he cut me off.

"No, you say you know…" he let out a puff of air, "but how many times have I told you, you should know the color, the type of car, if not the make and model, but at least the color, of the car behind you, without having to look in the rearview mirror."

"I didn't look," I began to protest, even though I knew it was futile.

"No, you're right," he admitted, crossing his arms over his chest. "You didn't look. But you weren't sure, either. You were guessing. You hadn't checked in a while." He rubbed a hand over his beard, or the start of one, at least. It was practically stubble now, but it would grow quickly. Dad kept his face clean shaven typically, for work, but he allowed himself the luxury of letting it go whenever we were on vacation. Mom liked to tease him about it, some little private joke that I didn't quite get. I had a feeling it was something sexual. I didn't really want to know.

I grimaced, and Dad caught my expression. Not having a clue where my random thought process had ended up, he sighed deeply, "I don't mean to be hard on you, Teddy." His voice was softer, gentler now. I didn't look at him, keeping my eyes fixed straight ahead. "You're a good kid." His arms relaxed, hands falling to his lap. "We'll go for your test when we get back home. Maybe..." he paused for a moment, "... in a few weeks. You still have plenty of time to get your license this year. Before you go away."

That had been the plan. I obviously wanted to have my driver's license before going away to college. That wasn't until next fall, though, more than plenty of time. It was only mid-November.

"Sounds good," I muttered gruffly, wanting to drop the topic. Dad seemed satisfied. He settled back in his seat, chin propped on one hand as he continued to stare out the window, eyes glazed over.

He had to be tired. He was coming off of a twelve-hour shift. He had been on-call and ended up at the hospital last night, as usual. Mom tried to suggest he rest, that we delay leaving for a day, or a half a day at least, so he could nap, but Dad had insisted he was fine. He'd insisted that I could drive most of the way so that he could sleep in the car. So much for that. I had seen him start to nod off a few times, but ultimately his need to watch me like a hawk had won the battle with his exhaustion.

Part of me still wished Mom had come with us. I had given her crap about it, made a fuss when she said she wasn't coming. I'd reminded her that she came last time. But that trip had been to Florida, in February. And more importantly, it hadn't been a hunting trip. She insisted that had nothing to do with it, but I knew better.

She had glanced sideways at Dad, busy at the stove, his back to us. I was sitting at the island. Mom leaned against the countertop, sipping her glass of wine. "Of course, I'll be bummed to miss out on seeing everyone again," she mused. Her eyes were on his back, as she spoke to me for his benefit. She did that a lot. "You'll have to say hi to Michelle and Sandy for me." She sipped contemplatively. "I bet the kids will all look so different. It's been how long now?"

"Almost three years," I murmured.

"Three years... wow." She gazed at me over the rim of her glass, her eyes sad. "Think how much you've grown in three years." She turned away from me. "They'll be practically unrecognizable."

"Isn't this the turn coming up?" Dad barked at me, pointing up ahead. I snapped out of it and peered at the sign on the corner up ahead on the right. *Hiddleston*. I switched on my turn signal and hit the brakes as smoothly as possible.

We drove in silence until we reached Groesbeck, but I could sense Dad eying me in a dissatisfied sort of way. I made sure I was paying attention this time and saw the turn well in advance.

We pulled into a gravel drive several minutes later. I scanned the address on the first house, just past the corner, and continued on to the second. The address was displayed across the top of the porch in large block numbers. There was a white truck parked in the driveway out front. A narrow strip of gravel led around the side of the house, promising more parking spots, but I opted to take the last spot out front. I wouldn't admit it, but I still wasn't super comfortable backing up over long distances. I didn't want to end up having to back up down that narrow drive when it was time to head out.

As we were getting out of the car, Dad clapped me on the shoulder and called something to me before slamming his door shut. I climbed out and stretched. My back and shoulders were tense, and my arms were a little sore.

It had been a beautiful drive for the past hour or two, at least. Our route had taken us through miles of rolling hills surrounded by fall colors. Although the colors here were clearly past their prime, the landscape more faded than it had been back home. One of the other docs had chosen the location for this trip. I thought it had been Dr. Montgomery. Our group rented out two houses, and I had been picturing them directly next to each other, but the houses seemed to be set far apart here. The other house was nowhere in sight, and I figured it must be somewhere up the road.

My gut clenched as the front door swung open. Dr. Montgomery stepped outside. "Teddy." I turned back to the road and saw Dad peeking at me from around the open trunk. "I asked you to help me with this. I need to move the gun case out of the way first."

"Sorry," I mumbled, trotting over to him. "I didn't hear you." I winced inwardly at the brief spasm crossing his features: guilt, sorrow, or a mix of the two. I felt a brief flare of anger burn in my chest in response.

"Sorry," he said, nodding down to the case in his hands. He had it halfway out of the trunk and was clearly struggling with the weight. "Can you grab the other end?"

I moved quickly around him and grasped the other end of the case. We lifted it together and set it down on the gravel a few feet away.

"Doctor!" I heard Dr. M's voice call out behind me. Dad straightened up, and his face broke out into a wide grin as he moved past me.

"Doctor!" He exclaimed back, and I turned to see him pulling Dr. Montgomery into a bear hug. They clapped each other on the back, laughing. "It's been far too long," Dad added.

Dr. Montgomery turned to me, grinning. "Teddy! Look at you, my God. I don't think I would have been able to pick you off the street. You've grown, what, a foot and a half at least, since I saw you last." He stretched his hand out to shake mine. I gripped it firmly.

"It's good to see you again Dr. Montgomery," I replied.

"Bah." He waved a hand. "Call me Craig, Teddy, there's no need for all that formality." I nodded, knowing I would do no such thing. "Evelyn's inside." He pointed back at the house. My gut twisted again slightly. "She and Ryan are trying to get the TV working." He looked over at Dad and rolled his eyes a bit, shrugging his shoulders. "I would think there are plenty of other more interesting things to do than watch TV out here, but heck, what do I know?"

Dad laughed and patted Dr. Montgomery on the back again. "Don't worry, they're going to get plenty of time out in nature this weekend. Let them watch some TV tonight, it'll give them something to do while we catch up."

"Cards tonight?" I heard Dr. M ask hopefully as they walked away towards the house. I glanced back at the car, and our forgotten bags. Dad had left the gun case just sitting out, too. That wasn't like him.

I sighed, and was about to call out to him, but decided to let it go. I'd remind him in a few minutes. I grinned a little to myself. As fun as it would be to give him shit about being irresponsible, I didn't think that would go over well. I grabbed our bags myself and slung one over each shoulder, following them up the walkway and the wooden stairs, and into the house.

Stepping through the threshold was like going back in time. The main floor had a sort of open concept. The kitchen was off to the left of the door, and did have a wall around it, with an alcove that opened into the dining table area. The main seating area was to the right of the dining table; a large couch spanning the middle of the room, next to a loveseat and armchair, a large square coffee table in the middle, framing a fireplace. The fireplace was bracketed by tall bookshelves on either side. Holding various worn paperbacks, glass bowls and vases, and knick-knacks. There was a sort of funky pattern on the couch and loveseat that reminded me of the 80s; a zigzagging pattern, like lightning, in teal, baby blue, and white.

A massive, old-fashioned TV cabinet sat to the right of the fireplace, partially blocking the bookshelf. The cabinet doors that normally hid the TV were swung open. Ryan stood in front of it, the TV half pulled out and twisted sideways. His upper torso was in the cabinet as he messed around with the wires in the back.

I looked around for Evelyn, but didn't see her. "Teddy!" I turned to see her bounding down the stairs with a book clutched in one hand. She was smiling at me, green eyes sparkling. Her copper hair fell in fuzzy ringlets in a halo down to her shoulders. She did look different. Her face was older; sharper and more angular somehow, but she was still just as beautiful as I remembered her being.

I grinned back at her. "Hey Ev, how's it going?" I set the bags down at my feet as she took the last few steps at a trot and came to a stop next to me. Her head barely came up to my chin.

"Oh you know." She rolled her eyes and dropped her voice a little lower. "I've been having so much fun already..." She glanced over at our dads, but they had moved into the kitchen and were ignoring us. She shook her head at me conspiratorially, glancing back over at Ryan. "We've spent the past half hour trying to get the TV working." She shrugged and held up her book. "I'm ready to give up at this point. How've you been?"

"Good." I nodded. I shrugged, flushing slightly when she stared at me expectantly, seeming to want me to say more.

"What have you been up to lately?" She pressed, lifting a hand up to tuck a curl behind her ear. It sprung back up again as soon as she let go.

"You know." I shrugged again, suddenly at a loss for words. I had never been good at small talk. "School. You know, this and that. Nothing too exciting. How about you?"

She grinned, and sighed, thinking for a moment, then held up her book, the cover facing away from me. "You know... a lot of this." She shrugged again. "There's not much going on this time of year." She shook her head, a frown on her face. "God I hate winter." I chuckled at her expression. "And snow." I sighed, nodding. "Do you think it will snow this weekend? It hasn't started up yet back at home, but it's been cold. You can tell it's coming."

I thought for a moment. "Well, the chance of snow is always higher, up in the mountains. It looked like they haven't gotten any yet, at least not recently, on the drive in though."

She nodded, a thoughtful expression on her face. "Well, I just threw some snacks together. Are you hungry?"

"Sure." I nodded. "I could eat."

She grinned at me like I'd said something witty, and motioned for me to follow her. I grabbed our bags and tucked them against a wall, following her around the couch. She plopped into the armchair to the left of the couch and motioned to the coffee table. There was a platter with cheese and crackers and salami. Some grapes and nuts too.

"Thanks," I said, "It looks great."

She smiled up at me. "There are some napkins there if you want one. Or there are little plates in the kitchen." She looked over at Ryan as I took a seat on the couch. "Teddy's here," she called over to him. Like he didn't already know.

I stared at the back of his varsity jacket. The '05 emblazoned across the back taking up most of the width of his broad shoulders, with 'The Falcons' written underneath in gold cursive.

Ryan gingerly shifted out of the cabinet, being careful not to hit his head, as he turned halfway towards me. "Hey," he muttered.

"Hey," I responded back. I didn't meet Evelyn's eyes, but I knew she was giving us a look. I reached out and grabbed a couple grapes. "Where's Katie?" I asked.

Ryan sighed. "I dunno... over at the house." He shrugged and sat down heavily on the loveseat, the metals hanging from the front of his jacket clinking together. I tried not to stare at them. I thought I saw some for swimming and possibly track. He was captain of the football team now, too. I had heard all about that earlier this fall. "She's hanging out with Mom for a bit. Getting things unpacked, or whatever." He waved a hand dismissively. "Dad ran up to the local grocery store to grab some *supplies*." He rolled his eyes, and grinned at Evelyn. I wasn't sure what 'supplies' referred to, but he had put it in air-quotes. Evelyn grinned at him then caught my expression.

"Alcohol," she said to me. "Well, he's grabbing bacon and eggs, and milk and stuff too, but mainly, alcohol."

I nodded. "Got it. My Dad brought a bunch with us. I'm sure they'll have more than enough."

Evelyn smirked. "You know how they are." She grabbed a grape and popped it in her mouth. She chewed for a moment, before continuing. My eyes dropped to her lips. There was something about the curve of her full lips that I found completely distracting. Her cheeks and nose were still peppered in the tiniest freckles. I tried not to stare, but I couldn't help it, mesmerized by her lips moving. "They're all excited to try whatever local beers." She shrugged. "Isn't a beer a beer? I bet they're all the same."

"You don't know?" Ryan sneered.

"What?" Her eyes lingered on me for a moment, as she caught me watching her. She tore them away and glanced over at Ryan. "Know what?"

"What beer tastes like, I mean." He raised an eyebrow at Evelyn. "Tell me you've tried beer before."

Evelyn rolled her eyes and crossed her arms over her chest. "Of course I have. It's not like I've gone and tried a ton of craft beers, but yes, I have tasted beer before, Ryan." She looked over at me, her lips pressed thin in annoyance.

Ryan was staring at me now. "What about you, Teddy?" Why did he have to say my name like that? Like it was ironic, somehow.

"You can just call me Ted, you know."

He raised an eyebrow at me, and ran a hand through his thick brown hair, lifting it off his forehead. "Oh yeah? Ted? But not Edwin, right?" He snorted a little. "Do you go by Edwin, back home?" I glared at him, keeping my expression smooth and flat.

"I know what my name is, actually, but thanks for the reminder."

He just stared at me, a hint of anger in his eyes. Of course he was mad. In my experience, bullies didn't like it when you gave them attitude. They liked it even less when you weren't afraid of them. I forced myself to meet his stare, refusing to blink no matter how much my eyes burned.

"Stop stalling and answer the question," he replied evenly.

"Really guys?" Evelyn let out an exasperated huff. "You've been together for, what, not even five minutes now? Give me a break."

I refused to look away from him. "Yes, Ryan, I've tasted beer before."

"Really? Someone offered you one? I find that hard to believe." He shrugged and stood up, going back over to the TV. The odds of him fixing it were pretty much non-existent. I didn't know why he was bothering.

"God this is going to be a long weekend," Evelyn murmured, tilting her head back and sighing deeply. "Can't you guys just skip the whole bickering thing this time and move straight to being friends again?"

I stared at the coffee table, my cheeks flushed slightly. I had been hoping that maybe Ryan had grown out of being a dick, but it sure wasn't looking like it.

"I'll be right back," I said, standing up and moving over to the kitchen. I didn't look back, although I could hear them saying something to each other. Probably talking about me. I decided I didn't want to know.

"Dad," I called out, walking into the kitchen. He was leaning against the counter, chatting with Dr. Montgomery and his wife, Michelle.

"Oh, hi Teddy." She smiled over at me as she saw me entering. "It's so nice to see you again. Look at you," she crooned, and pulled me in for a hug. I hugged her back loosely. When she let go, she touched my hair with her fingertips. "I love your hair." She looked over at my Dad. "It's longer, but it looks nice. I like it." She turned back to me and winked.

Great. So Dad had been complaining about my hair to them. I wore it a little longer; it had grown out just past my ears now. "Thanks Mrs. Montgomery." I managed to grin back at her. "Mom says hi, and she's sorry she couldn't make it this time."

She smiled at me and squeezed my hand. "Thank you, Teddy. We'll miss her this weekend." She sighed. "Just means we'll have to plan another trip, sooner rather than later!" She turned back to the counter, rummaging in a drawer.

"Um Dad, we left the gun case sitting out on the driveway. We should probably go move it."

"Oh jeez." He jumped back from the counter. "Thanks Teddy." He shook his head. "I didn't mean to leave it there. I got distracted by this idiot." He gestured back at Dr. Montgomery, who just laughed and turned to open the fridge. He pulled out a beer bottle and started searching in another drawer, presumably for a bottle opener. Mrs. Michelle handed him one, arm raised, without turning to look at him.

"Ah ha!" Dr. M exclaimed, taking it. "Thank you, my dear." He tipped his head towards Dad as he peeled the cap off the bottle and tossed it onto the counter. "I'm grabbing one for you, too. We're not waiting on Dave to start drinking. That man is a human slug." I snorted. "I'm still shocked he manages not to kill all his patients."

"Craig..." Mrs. Michelle murmured, shaking her head.

Dr. M just winked at me. "You should have seen him in med school– we called him Dr. Slo-mo."

Dad let out a barking laugh and clapped me on the back. "Come on, let's go take care of it." I followed him out of the kitchen.

Evelyn was curled up in the armchair with her book open. Dad saw her sitting there and called a greeting over to her, waving as he headed over to the door. She smiled and waved back. "Hi Dr. Ellsworth," she called. She watched me for a moment, expression serious, then looked over in Ryan's direction. I turned away and followed Dad outside.

We made quick work of lifting the heavy gun case back into the trunk. Dad made sure the car was locked. The gun case itself was locked too, so it hardly mattered. I glanced around us. We were surrounded by trees. Some golden and brown hues, and faded reds, well past their prime, mixed in with bare tree branches and evergreens. A thick carpet of leaves covered the ground. Other than the house we passed on the corner, and the one Ryan's family was renting, I wondered if there were any other neighbors around. A stretch of woods ran alongside the road on the other side of the street; nothing but trees for as far as I could see. The odds of someone walking past and walking off with our gun case seemed slim to none.

Dad nodded at me. "Thanks Ted. It completely slipped my mind." I nodded back at him. "Hey, do you want to do some target practice later?" He nodded towards the back of the house. "We have permission to shoot on the property. Craig brought some targets with him. Might be good for Evelyn and Ryan. I'm not sure how much experience they have."

I shrugged nonchalantly. "Yeah, I guess."

He studied me for a moment before patting me on the shoulder. "It might give you a chance to show off a little." He grinned at me and jerked his head towards the house. I felt my cheeks flush, and looked away towards the tree line. "What?" he was still grinning at me. I just shook my head and rolled my eyes. "Come on, you're an ace. No reason not to show off a little." He shrugged. "But hey, you do you, son."

I cringed inwardly and hoped he would stop talking. He turned and headed back into the house, and I fell behind him gratefully. "If not today, we can tomorrow. Obviously, we're planning on hunting first thing in the morning, but we could always do some target practice tomorrow afternoon or evening. Although, anyone else hunting in the vicinity might not appreciate that. Too much of a racket, and we risk scaring all the deer away." I gazed up at the trees surrounding us. They loomed over the house, forming a sort of canopy.

I thought for a moment. "Shouldn't we be worried about that tonight, then?"

Dad paused for a second, then waved his hand. "Nah, I don't think there's much harm in it tonight. There's not much around here, but I doubt anyone would actually be hunting in the immediate vicinity. Mount Snow is just up the road, and this is all private property. Not to mention, opening day is technically tomorrow. But," he shrugged, "if no one feels up for it tonight, it would probably be fine tomorrow afternoon."

"You planning on getting a deer right away then?" I grinned a little.

"Ha!" He half turned, grinning back at me. "Of course I am Teddy."

We entered the house again as Dr. M was stepping out of the kitchen. "What? You talking about bagging a deer first thing?" They moved over to the dining table as he handed Dad a beer. They started giving each other shit about hunting tomorrow. I moved to head back over to the couch, but I stopped on the way to grab a book out of my bag. I was glad I'd thought to bring one; didn't seem like there would be much else to do tonight.

"You're coming with us tomorrow, right Teddy?" Dr. Montgomery called out to me. "You and Ryan too, right?" He grinned over at Evelyn. "Ev has already promised to join us."

"Begrudgingly," Evelyn added, raising her eyebrows without glancing up from her book.

"Begrudgingly," Dr. Montgomery repeated with a chuckle. "That's right."

"I'm definitely in," Ryan spoke up, eyes on me. He had apparently given up on the TV and was splayed out across the loveseat.

"Do you have your hunting license Ryan?" Dad asked. He was a stickler for the rules. No way Ryan was going without one.

Ryan nodded, and called out, "Yeah, Dad and I took care of all that before we left. Katie doesn't. She still says she wants to tag along though." He looked back over at me, as I continued to dig through my bag, and his voice dropped lower. "You could hang back with her, Teddy." He grinned.

"I'm going," I said, turning to Dr. M, ignoring Ryan pointedly. "I got my license too."

He nodded approvingly at me. "Good." He turned to Dad. "Maybe we should do some target practice today after all. It'd probably be more helpful than waiting until tomorrow."

Dad nodded his agreement and took another sip of his beer. Mrs. Michelle glanced at her watch. "Where is Dave? It really shouldn't have taken him that long to grab the few things on the list."

"You know him," Dr. Montgomery chuckled, "Dr. Slo-mo, like I said. He's probably just taking his sweet time." He glanced at his watch as well. "We'll be on track to get dinner going; if we still want to eat early, that is." He shrugged. "We don't have to wait for him to get started." Mrs. Michelle nodded, looking reassured. I finished rooting around in my bag, my hand finally landing on my dog-eared copy of *Dune*. I plopped down on the couch and pulled out the bookmark, setting it down next to me.

"Dune!" Evelyn called over to me, "I just read that earlier this fall. Isn't it good?"

"Yeah." I nodded, grinning over at her, "I've read it like, several times." I shrugged. "It's one of my favorites."

Ryan snorted, eying the cover. "Doesn't look very interesting."

I shrugged at him. "Well, it's a classic."

"Doesn't mean it's any good. We've read a bunch of classics in school. Most of them suck." Evelyn sighed; a disapproving look on her face.

"I like the classics. And I like pretty much everything we've read in school." I shrugged. "Shakespeare, *Lord of the Flies*, *The Crucible-*"

"That's cause you're pretentious, Teddy," Evelyn quipped. But she was grinning at me, a fond warmth in her eyes.

Ryan chuckled darkly at her comment. "I couldn't get through any of those. They were all terrible."

"Yeah? What was the last book you read that you liked?" It was a genuine question; I was actually curious what sort of books a person like Ryan would read. But he glared at me, his cheeks flushing slightly as though I'd insulted him.

He seemed at a loss for a response for once. Evelyn waited for him to answer, an expectant look on her face. He looked back and forth between us, and I could sense the predicament I'd put him in.

I could tell he hadn't read anything recently. And he probably wanted to call me a nerd, bash me for liking books, but he clearly knew that Evelyn was an avid reader, too. He couldn't make fun of me without putting her down at the same time. And there was no way he would do that.

As much of a jerk as Ryan could be at times, he had always been careful, in the past, to not extend that asshole behavior towards Evelyn. The thought that he might like her, hit me suddenly in the gut, as though I'd been punched.

He stammered for a moment, "Well, I've been too busy with sports lately to do much reading. We just wrapped up football season, obviously, and I'm the captain, and now I have swimming." He shrugged nonchalantly, regaining his composure. "I don't have the time."

I nodded thoughtfully at him. "But you do this weekend, right?" I held up my worn-out copy of *Dune*, eyebrows raised. "Like I said, I've read this multiple times. If you want to borrow it, feel free." Ryan just stared at me for a moment.

I looked over to see Evelyn grinning, a mischievous sort of look on her face as she watched us. "Yeah, that would be cool, Ryan. Then we could all talk about it."

Ryan turned to her and then back to me, his cheeks starting to turn red again. He shrugged, clearing his throat. "Yeah, I mean, we've got a lot going on this weekend. But yeah, I could read some of it, I guess."

I picked up the bookmark and set it back in place. Just then, I heard a voice call out from behind me. "Teddy!" Katie moved swiftly around the couch, making a beeline for me. I managed to stand just in time to get practically knocked over backward as she barreled into me, throwing her arms around me and squeezing me in a hug.

"Hi Katie." I hugged her back and couldn't help but grin. She released me a moment later and went to flop down on the far end of the couch. I caught the icy look that Ryan gave me as I took a seat.

She unzipped her coat, and started pulling off her hat, revealing her long blonde hair piled in a messy bun on top of her head. She unwrapped the knit scarf she was wearing, folded several times around her neck, as she panted slightly. "God, I'm dying in this. Mom made me bundle up like it's the dead of winter. It's barely even chilly outside. I got all sweaty walking over here. You know, it's farther than I realized." She pointed to her right, "We're about a half mile up the road that way. You should come back and check out our place Teddy."

"No way that's a half mile," Ryan grumbled. "Might be a quarter of a mile at best."

Katie looked around the room. "Our living room is a little bigger than this, I don't know why we're hanging out here. We should go back there after dinner. You should see my room. Where are you all sleeping?" She peered up at the ceiling, and I followed her gaze. A half wall was visible above us; it looked like the stairs led to some kind of loft area.

"Ooh, that looks fun," Katie murmured. "How long was your drive Teddy? Ours took *for-ev-er*." She drew out the last few syllables in a groan. Katie kept up a running dialogue consisting of her stream of consciousness, as was usually her way. She was about four years younger than us; probably just turned fourteen or was just about to. She was a sweet kid. The four of us had spent countless vacations running around together, the three of us getting into whatever shenanigans we had planned while Katie tagged along behind us.

Ryan treated his little sister with a grudging tolerance, on most occasions, Evelyn was of course nothing but kind to her. Katie had always loved hanging out with me. I suspected mainly because I was so quiet. I hated talking, and she never stopped. I was a benevolent audience, that rarely interrupted, whose silence was taken for agreement in all matters. I didn't have any siblings, so Katie was probably the closest thing to a little sister I would ever experience.

I'd lost track for a moment of what she was saying, but she continued on, chattering all about the drive here, and how she wasn't going to hunt tomorrow, but she was going with us, because she did want to see what it was like, but she didn't want to see a deer actually get shot. That would be way too disturbing.

Evelyn met my gaze and we grinned at each other at that last statement. She stood and grabbed a napkin, setting some crackers and cheese on it and handing it over to Katie. "Here Katie, have a snack." She looked over in our dad's direction. "I think it might be a while until dinner."

Katie took the napkin carefully. "Oh, thank you, I'm starving, actually." She busied herself with snacking, which slowed her commentary down considerably.

Evelyn settled back into the armchair, tucking her feet underneath her and opening her book again. I stared down at *Dune*, still gripped in my hands. I thought about handing it over to Ryan, but decided I didn't want to get into it with him again. Ryan stood up after a moment and wandered over to the French glass doors behind Evelyn's chair. He gazed out into the trees behind the house as Katie spoke. It looked like there was a small balcony out there.

I stared over at the empty fireplace. I figured it was a gas fireplace. I tried not to stare at Evelyn, but my gaze kept wandering back to her involuntarily. I had been nervous to see her again; worried that it would be weird between us. It had been so long. But we had seemingly picked up right where we left off. She hadn't changed much, in all reality.

She was wearing an oversized hoodie that hung on her narrow frame. It occurred to me with a lurch in my stomach to wonder if it belonged to someone else. Maybe a boyfriend back home. She wore tight leggings. My eyes wandered over the curves of her thighs. I cleared my throat.

"Does the fireplace work?" I asked during a small gap in Katie's never-ending monologue.

Evelyn looked up, eying the fireplace quizzically. "I'm not sure actually." She looked over towards where her parents sat with Dad.

"We should try it out tonight." She checked her watch and looked over at me. "Are we doing target practice before or after dinner?"

I shrugged, looking outside. "Before would probably be better, for light. I don't know how early it gets dark here." Ryan was nodding in agreement, his back to us still.

Dad seemed to have been listening in on our conversation because he stood up and announced he was going to go get started early on dinner. Evelyn's parents offered to help, and the three of them headed into the kitchen, taking their drinks with them.

Evelyn smiled over at me for a moment, before returning to her book.

"What are you reading?" I asked her. She shrugged, and closed the book over her thumb, looking down at the cover.

"I dunno, it's sort of a... romance novel. Not a classic." She shrugged again, cheeks flushing. I felt my curiosity pique.

"Oh yeah? Is it any good so far?"

She grinned, biting down on her bottom lip as she looked back down at the book. "Yeah, it's okay so far." She seemed to think for a moment, about to add something else. But she flushed again slightly and seemed to think better of it, shaking her head and grinning to herself. She pulled the collar of her hoodie up, tucking it over her mouth, and propping her chin in her hand. She held the book open in her other hand; the cover facing away from me. I leaned to the side, trying to angle to see the cover, but she saw me out of her periphery, and twisted the book further away from me, giggling a little. I started laughing.

"What the heck Ev," I started, but she just shook her head and laughed harder, still covering her mouth with her hoodie.

"I'm here, I'm here!" I turned to see Ryan and Katie's dad, Dr. Carter, stepping through the door, laden with grocery bags, as a cool gust of air washed over us. Ryan moved over quickly to help him. "Thanks Ry," he said, somewhat out of breath, "There's a bunch more in the truck.

I stood and went to help as well, leaning over Evelyn as I moved past her. She peered up at me in surprise, her green eyes wide. "We'll finish this conversation later," I murmured to her.

"We absolutely will not," she retorted back. Her voice was muffled, but I could still hear the grin behind her words.

2

—·—

We walked in a line, single file, weaving between trees. The light was already starting to fade a bit, leaving us a narrow window of time for target practice.

Dr. M had set up a few targets in a clearing a ways back from the house while Dad and I grabbed the shotguns. Dad typed in the code; *32475,* I chanted in a sing-song rhythm in my head, as he flicked the latches open with a loud *clunk-clunk.*

He flipped the lid open, and I stared into the gun case for a moment as he started to remove our shotguns. "Jesus Dad," I murmured, "why did you bring so many guns?" He looked at me sideways. "Did the deer organize into a militia? Are they storming the gates?"

He huffed the breath of a laugh at that, despite himself. "I just grabbed the case Ted, it wasn't on purpose. I store all of these together."

"Wait, when did you get this handgun? Sweet." I reached into the case to grab the handle of a slick black handgun, but I felt his hand on my arm, stopping me.

"Yeah, it's not a toy Teddy. How many times have we had that conversation."

"Okay Dad," I chuckled, holding my hands up in the air in an 'I surrender' sort of motion. "I am definitely aware of that. Forget it." And yes, I thought, to him, these guns absolutely were toys, but it wasn't worth triggering another lecture.

"Okay," Dad continued, grabbing a box of shells and shutting and locking the case. He pulled our hearing protection from a bag as well. "I think we have everything we need. Let's go." Thankfully he was in a good mood tonight.

We trailed behind the others. Evelyn carried her rifle awkwardly as though she didn't quite feel comfortable holding it. Dad had allowed me to carry my shotgun, at least. Well, it wasn't *my* shotgun, just the one I normally used. Dad liked to take me to the range. We'd done targets for a while, then moved on to clays eventually. He thought of it as some sort of bonding ritual between us, I was sure of that, but he was also somewhat of an amateur survivalist. Not the bunker kind, but he took it fairly seriously.

It started, I think, with a somewhat unhealthy obsession with zombies. Zombie movies and books, moving on to general dystopian thrillers from there. I remembered Mom had protested me watching them with him, at first, but she had given in reluctantly, rolling her eyes and shaking her head at us as she went to go hang out in another room. I could tell from her smile that she was secretly pleased we were spending time together.

He went on a sort of a 'what would you do if the world ended' kick for a while. The downside of it was a lot of redundant conversations about how to find your way in the woods, how to make water safe to drink, how to build a shelter... but the upside had been a lot of camping trips, target practice, boy scout-type classes, and him generally spending time with me. He had limited free time, like most physicians, and he was always tired, but he also couldn't seem to sit still, as a general rule.

I hung back and fell into line last as we made our way out to the clearing. I'd had a sort of awkward, embarrassing moment just after dinner, and didn't really feel like interacting with anyone right now.

It had just been so loud in the house. The small space full of people, everyone talking over each other at once, dishes clanging as the table was cleared. Ryan was teasing Katie, throwing her little purse over her head, too high for her to grab, then managing to get to it first before she could snatch it back. I got sick of it, eventually; I stood and shot an arm in the air and managed to grab it.

Ryan's eyebrows went up, and he ran at me, tackling me onto the couch. Before I knew it we were basically in a full on wrestling match. I could hear Katie and Evelyn yelling at him to stop.

"Wow, look at you, Teddy..." he grinned at me. "You been lifting?" His voice dropped low. "You're not such a little dweeb anymore, huh? You put some muscle on."

"Shut the fuck up, Ryan," I muttered back. "You know I've kicked your ass before. More than once."

He'd burst out laughing at that. "Yeah," he said, still grinning. "But I kicked your ass right back."

I managed to shrug as he got me in a headlock. "I guess that's accurate."

I got the upper hand eventually, flipping him onto the floor. He landed on his back between the couch and the coffee table, and I fell on top of him, purse flying out of both of our hands. Katie ran to scoop it up as Ryan let out an "Oof" that made me grin as the air got knocked out of him.

He started laughing again, and before I knew it we were both cracking up, too weak to fight at the moment. "God damn it Teddy. Get the fuck off me man, I can't breathe," he managed to rasp out.

I stood up and offered him a hand, helping to pull him to his feet. Evelyn was shaking her head at us, grinning in a satisfied way. "You two are idiots."

We sat down to rest for a moment, but the relative peace hadn't lasted very long. I'd settled in to read, trying to block out all the noise, but Ryan got bored and grabbed the purse again a few minutes later. Katie made a big fuss this time.

She was whining and yelling at him to stop. Evelyn chimed in too. The adults were all laughing. I could feel that irrational anger that I'd managed to tamp down starting to build in my chest, buzzing in my head until I couldn't take it anymore.

I'd stood up suddenly, rushing to leave the room. I wasn't paying attention, and I ran into Evelyn's Mom, knocking the armful of dirty dishes out of her hands. Food went everywhere, and two plates were broken. That had been bad enough, but it was made worse by the fact that Evelyn and Ryan had both seen me; seen my face as I rushed to leave. I knew they could tell I was upset, that something was wrong.

A dead silence had fallen for a moment, Mrs. Michelle watching me, a concerned look in her eyes that made me feel worse. My shoulders rose and fell, and I knew I was panting slightly, breathing too hard. Evelyn said softly, "Why don't you go sit upstairs, Teddy. It's probably a bit quieter up there." I hadn't even turned to look at her. I couldn't. I forced myself to walk slowly and calmly upstairs, my heart pounding in my chest.

I heard them murmuring to each other afterwards their voices soft, all the noise and chaos subdued. I sat on the couch upstairs, hands folded together. I couldn't sit still, though. I could feel that irrational anger turning into panic. Anxiety started to creep in, like an old, unwanted friend that just couldn't take a hint.

I needed to move. I took deep breaths, rocking forward and backwards slightly. I hated this. I hated this about myself. The panic never had a real cause, never had a reason. I would get overwhelmed, or sometimes even underwhelmed, and it would strike out of nowhere. I couldn't do this right now, not in front of all of them. I wished desperately for my Discman; it was in my bag downstairs, with the set of oversized headphones that Mom had found for me. Sometimes music worked to calm me down. But I couldn't go back down there to get it.

Eventually, Evelyn made her way upstairs. I heard soft footfalls on the stairs and knew it had to be either her or Katie, coming to check on me. Thankfully I had managed to calm down a bit by then.

I'd taken the time to stand up and study the room as I paced around. Sometimes, focusing on things I could see, my surroundings, helped, but other times it made it worse.

There was an old faded blue couch against the far wall, across from the stairs. A smaller TV cabinet in the adjacent corner, with what looked like an old Nintendo hooked up to it. I saw only one controller though. The door next to it opened up into a bathroom. The wooden ceiling was slanted, a triangle angling towards the peak of the roof.

It felt cozy up here, like a warm little nest. I stood in front of the couch, studying the large painting that hung above it. It took up most of the wall. It looked like a painting for kids, but it was clearly also a map of sorts. It showed Mount Snow: the local ski mountain. I knew it was close by, and adjacent to the Green Mountain National Forest, where we would be hunting tomorrow.

The painting showed the different ski trails, each one labeled, some of them seeming to join up, crisscrossing. Little skiers with smiling faces and rosy cheeks peppered the mountain face. There was a ski lodge at the bottom of the mountain. People were hanging around there, drinking cups of hot cocoa. The ski lift had a little line of people waiting for their turn. It was very detailed. Enough to distract me.

I turned to see Evelyn approaching around the corner of the stairs. She gave me a tentative smile, then nodded towards the painting. "It's cute, isn't it." She came and stood next to me. I willed myself to stay calm. The panic was still there, but it was starting to fade thankfully. Just a background hum now.

"You okay, Teddy?" she asked, dropping her voice lower. I didn't look at her.

"Yeah, I'm fine," I retorted back, my voice coming out somewhat more gruff than I had intended. "I just..." I trailed off, no plan for what I was going to say next. It wasn't like I could explain it. I'd always been this way. As a little kid I'd cry or throw a tantrum. Now, I just went away on my own, and had stupid little rituals to help calm myself down. It didn't happen as much now, thankfully. Just my dumb luck that it would on this trip, in front of her.

"I know..." Evelyn started, then stopped abruptly. She trailed off, clearly unsure what to say as well. I glanced at her sideways for a moment, trying to think of something to say.

"Do you still want to come target shooting with us?" she asked me. A hopeful uplift to her voice. I studied her for a moment before answering, running a hand through my hair. Little lines creased the pale skin between her brows. Her eyebrows were a pretty copper-brown, matching her frizzy curls, her green eyes framed by tiny auburn freckles. Her skin looked so soft; a pale creamy-white. I thought about what it would feel like to stroke a hand across her cheek.

"Yeah, Ev, I still want to come," I managed to respond, and her lips parted in a satisfied smile. I was wrong; she had changed. She had been cute. Pretty, before. Now she was truly beautiful. So beautiful it hurt.

My chest ached as I turned away from her. I flopped down on the couch, putting my chin in my hands, elbows propped on my knees. "I'm sorry about the dishes. The mess. I'll go tell your Mom..."

"She already knows." Evelyn waved a hand. "Forget about it. It took all of ten seconds to clean up." She bit her bottom lip. "Um, I think we're getting ready to head out in a few minutes. I just wanted to make sure you didn't miss it."

I nodded and smiled up at her. "Great. I'll be down in a minute." She smiled back at me, nodding, and turned to head back down the stairs. She turned back once to look at me, pausing on the landing mid-way up. She caught me still watching her, and gave me a fleeting wide-eyed look that I couldn't interpret, before she disappeared around the corner.

I'd apologized anyway to Mrs. Montgomery when I got downstairs. She'd waved my apology away with both hands, patting me on the arm. "Oh Teddy, you never have to apologize, sweetie." She'd given me a long look, then turned away and went back to clearing up the kitchen. "Get going now; the others are already outside. I told your Dad I'd send you out when you were ready."

I watched Dad's back, as he moved through the trees in front of me. Dad and I never talked about it. About how I was. We sort of skirted around the issue. But I'd overheard him talking to Mom about it before. He called it my *sensitivity*. He talked about it like it was an object; something I owned. Or maybe more like an extra appendage I had, growing out of my body. He'd say things like, "Well, Teddy has his *sensitivity*. That'll get in the way of him participating in soccer."

Mom and I had talked about it before, quite a few times. She always brushed it away. Told me I was just different, but it was okay. Told me it was normal. A phase. Something I'd probably grow out of. But I didn't think so. It was a part of me. It just... was.

Mom found my 'differences', as she liked to call them, useful, too, in ways that Dad didn't. She'd always debrief with me after family parties, chatting in the car on the way home, my Dad stoic and silent, grunting noncommittally in answer to her questions. She'd turn to me, in the backseat, and say, 'I think cousin Patty has a gambling problem, don't you Teddy? Did you hear the way she talked about going to the casino?' Or, 'I think they're going to end up divorced. What did you think, Teddy? Did you see the way he was looking at her at dinner?'

Mom always wanted to hear what I thought about people. She said I noticed things, and that I was more observant than most. I used to think of it as something special about me, something magical almost. Sort of like a superpower that no one else had. I possessed a kind of premonition, a pre-knowing that couldn't be based in anything but the supernatural. I liked that thought. Like I was a character in one of the books I read, about to get whisked away into a magical realm, where I would find out I was secretly special all along. I would finally have a reason for why I was different.

I will never forget the last time I saw my Aunt Maria. We'd gone to visit my Grandma; she was getting older, and her health wasn't great and she'd started to get confused, Dad explained to me. She didn't quite seem to know where, or when, she was. Sometimes she didn't recognize the people around her. I thought about that a lot back then, what that would feel like. To wake up and think you were 25, only to look in the mirror, and see the face of an old woman, staring back. She'd chatted with me, while the adults all talked about cousins and distant relatives, and their old neighbors. My Grandma sat there grinning, rocking back and forth, her hands clasped over her knees. She told me about the tame owl that used to come visit them when she was a kid. How they left food for him, and eventually he would come land on her arm, eat right out of her hand. I murmured and nodded back to her, wondering if anything she was telling me was actually true.

My Aunt Maria was staying with her at the time and taking care of her. She lived close by and was retired. When I was a little kid, she always used to have candy for me, when we came to visit. Once she forgot, and she insisted on driving me up to the local grocery store, so I could pick something out. She had a great sense of humor, was always making a joke about something, making the whole room laugh.

We'd had a nice, normal visit, playing cards, and sitting in the living room, chatting, until Dad stood up and said it was time to get going. I'd given Grandma a hug and held on longer than usual. I said goodbye to Aunt Maria and gave her a quick hug as well.

Aunt Maria watched from the porch, standing in the doorway as we piled into the car at the curb. She was smiling, calling something out to my parents. I sat in the back seat, watching out the window.

As we pulled away, she stayed out on the porch, waving at me as I peered through the window. We made it past the next house, stopped at the corner, and turned right. I'd turned backward in my seat, watching her disappear through the rear window. I started crying, tears streaming down my face.

I wanted to call out to my Dad, wanted to scream at him to stop the car, to pull over. I pictured myself doing it, my heart in my throat. I pictured leaping out of the car, running across the road, back to her. Because I knew. I knew with certainty, in that moment, that I would never see her again.

I said nothing, though, because it made no sense. Grandma was the one who was sick. The one everyone was worried about. And I wouldn't be able to rationalize it, wouldn't be able to explain why I made them stop the car. I wiped my tears discreetly and pretended like nothing had happened. Calming myself down on the drive home.

I thought nothing of it, forgot about it, for a while. About a month or so later, Dad told me that Aunt Maria had lung cancer. It was advanced, and she likely wasn't going to make it. May not have much time left. She had been a practically life-long smoker. She was dead within two weeks.

I used to think that kind of knowing, knowing things before they happened, was magic, but now I knew better.

There was nothing magical about it. Mom was right; I was just observant. I'd thought about that day often. About Aunt

Maria standing on the porch, waving, watching us drive away, and I finally figured it out: I knew, because *she* knew. She must have known something was wrong. Knew she was sick. That it was bad. Maybe she didn't want to face it. Couldn't make herself go in. I don't know. But I only knew it because she did, and I saw it on her face.

I picked up on people's body language. Their expressions, their tone of voice, the things they said, but more importantly, the things they didn't say. That was all. I wasn't special. Just different. Just strange.

But, I made a promise to myself, after that. I would never ignore that feeling again. That gut feeling that told me with cold certainty something I couldn't or shouldn't possibly know. Even if it made no sense, even if it made people think I was strange, I would never keep silent again.

We shuffled along quietly, coats *swish-swishing* as we moved back and forth. The air held a bite to it that hadn't been there earlier in the afternoon. We entered a large clearing to see four rounded targets set up at the far edge of the treeline. The first target was the closest, with the last one set a few feet into the woods.

Dr. M was there waiting for us. "Who's first?" he asked, rubbing his gloved hands together. Evelyn and I looked at each other. Ryan raised his hand immediately, stepping forward. He held a rifle in one hand.

They helped him get set up; his dad passed him a handful of cartridges and a pair of earmuffs. I hung back at the treeline. As Ryan moved over to the first target, Dad came over and handed me a pair of earmuffs. I reached up and pulled my hearing aids out with one hand, the world suddenly going quiet. I pulled the battery doors open to the first click, so they wouldn't whistle in my pocket. I shoved them into the front pocket of my jeans and pulled on the earmuffs.

I looked up to see Evelyn watching me, her expression open, curious. Behind her, Ryan slid the final cartridge into place. He was eyeing me as well, a self-satisfied smirk on his face. It made me want to punch him in the throat.

Dad walked over to him. He was pointing and gesturing. Everyone turned to look at him. I couldn't make out what he was saying, not with my hearing aids off and earmuffs on, but I knew him well enough to know what he was doing; he was giving his safety speech, reminding everyone how to handle a gun properly. Apparently, he thought I didn't need a refresher. That, or he forgot I wouldn't be able to hear him.

Dr. Montgomery and Dr. Carter were standing off to the side, nodding, and interjecting something occasionally. Finally, Ryan squared up to the target, lifting the rifle to his shoulder. He seemed to be taking his time aiming. I jumped slightly at the first blast, chuckling a little as he was knocked a step backward from the recoil.

Ryan was a decent shot, although he tended to pull to the left. He missed the last two targets entirely, cheeks flushed red. He looked like he was pulling the trigger, not squeezing it. I watched as Dad stepped forward, giving him pointers. When he was done, Evelyn turned back to me, eyebrows raised, asking me something. I pulled one earmuff off. "What?" I asked, stepping forward, tilting my exposed ear towards her.

"Do you want to go next?" she repeated, stepping closer to me.

I shook my head. "Go ahead." Her smile was half grimace. She looked a little nervous. "Ladies first," I said, grinning back. Her smile broadened at that, although she gave me a look, sighing and moving over to the first target. I popped my earmuff back on.

Evelyn rushed. She didn't take her time sighting in, and her first shot went wide. Dad was distracted, chatting and laughing with Dr. M and Dr. C. Ryan hung a few feet behind Ev. His back was to me, but I could see his arms moving as he gestured to her. He walked over as she squared up to the target, and wrapped his arms around hers, adjusting her stance. I rolled my eyes, gritting my teeth as I watched them. Ryan stepped back, and Evelyn took another shot. She hit the target this time, on the far right.

I hung back and let Dr. C go next. He had been drinking beer at dinner, but he seemed steady. He was a decent shot as well, better than Ryan. Dad waved a hand and declined going next, gesturing at me to come forward. I moved forward and took the shells he handed me. Ryan turned to Evelyn and whispered something in her ear, his lips turning up in a wicked curve, his eyes never leaving mine. Dad clapped me on the back and backed up a few steps as I settled in front of the first target.

I'd sighted in my shotgun again before we left, but there was always a chance it had gotten jostled on the trip. I lifted the shotgun, falling into my familiar stance, muscle memory taking over. I braced myself for the kick-back as I leveled on the first target. I saw Ryan's face flash in my mind, the shit-eating grin as he whispered about me in Evelyn's ear, his arms wrapped around her.

I took the first shot, and it hit true; a dark hole appeared in the red center. I didn't pause, swiveling to my right, lining up the next target, and letting off another shot. It hit home and I pivoted again, shifting to the third, and then the final target. It was nearing dusk now, but I could see the target clearly visible from here; there wasn't much by way of underbrush on the edge of the clearing.

Four targets. Four dark holes. Near dead center. I turned to find Ryan and Evelyn staring at me, Ryan's jaw dropped slightly open. I eyed him, my face expressionless, and moved back to the treeline.

Dad stood next to Dr. M and Dr. C, and they stared at me as well. Dad stood with his arms crossed, a broad, satisfied smile on his face. His dark eyes twinkled in amusement. I pulled the earmuffs off.

"Holy shit," Dr. Carter murmured, looking from Dad to me, then back again. "Where'd you learn to shoot like that?"

Dad grinned as I just shrugged. "I've been taking him to the range the past couple years. He's gotten a decent amount of practice in, but he's always had a knack for it."

"I guess so," Dr. C replied, chuckling. "You should compete Teddy; you could win a decent amount of money, shooting like that."

I shrugged again, sighing. Dad was already nodding. "That's what I've been telling him. He won't do it." He exchanged a look with them. "Not to mention, Meg... doesn't like him shooting. She's always stressed about his..." he trailed off, pointing to his ear. "His ears, you know." He grinned over at me. "We're under strict orders to use hearing protection at all times. Right Teddy?"

I nodded, tight-lipped and set my shotgun down, leaning it against a tree. I stood with my hands in my jacket pockets.

"Are we ready to head back?" Dad asked, surveying the group. "Anyone else going?"

Dr. M shrugged. "And follow that performance? Are you kidding me?" He grinned at me. "Let's pack it up." He looked up at the sky. A crescent moon was just faintly visible, peeking over the crown of trees that circled us. "Besides, it's starting to get dark."

I helped carry two of the targets back, tucking them under one arm. I had left my hearing aids in my pocket and didn't hear Evelyn move up behind me. She spoke suddenly behind my right shoulder.

"I didn't know you could shoot like that Teddy. That was crazy."

I glanced over at her and shrugged. "Yeah," I chuckled a little. "Like Dad said, I've had a lot of practice. Anyone can learn to do it."

She was quiet for a moment, eying me. "I seriously doubt that."

I didn't respond back, dropping my eyes to the ground, watching for tree roots. I couldn't help but feel a little smug, though. At least I'd wiped the smile off Ryan's face.

"Hey," she said, nudging my arm with her elbow. "I bet you get the first deer tomorrow."

"We'll see." I shrugged, chuckling a little. "I'm actually not a big fan of hunting."

"Really?" she looked up at me in surprise.

"Yeah. I dunno." I looked up at the swiftly darkening sky for a moment. The wind gusted suddenly, tree branches swaying around us. The cool night air held a hint of damp earth, petrichor: the smell just before it rained. I breathed in deeply, the forest around us suddenly feeling foreign, the shadows ominous. Foreboding, almost. I peered into the depths but could no longer see more than a few feet in either direction. I was glad we would be back to the house soon. "I guess I've never liked killing anything." I looked down at her as she watched me. Studied me. I shrugged, "Even bugs." She laughed a little at that, her face growing serious again as I continued. "Have you ever killed a deer?" I asked. "Been there when one was dying?"

Her green eyes widened slightly. "No," she murmured. "I guess I haven't."

I nodded, looking back at my feet. "It's very... real. Not like how it feels in movies, or a book. It's..." I trailed off. "I've never told anyone this. Dad and I have gone hunting together loads of times. But... it always makes me feel a little sick," I admitted. I cleared my throat and shrugged. "If I see a deer tomorrow, maybe

I'll take a shot, maybe I won't." I looked back at her, her pretty little upturned nose flushed red. "If I don't..." I shrugged, "Or if I miss, well, that's why."

Her lips stretched in a smile, "And only I'll know."

I felt a bubble of warmth expand in my gut at her words. "Yeah," I murmured back, grinning, eyes locked on hers. "It'll be our secret." Her smile broadened, and I thought her cheeks looked flushed, but it was probably from the cold. She looked away from me, and we walked the rest of the way back to the house in a comfortable silence.

3

— · —

Mrs. Michelle and Mrs. Sandy were curled up on the couch in the living room when we got back, a glass of wine in hand. Katie was sitting in the armchair Evelyn had vacated, watching a movie. She'd somehow managed to get the TV working. She jumped up and rushed over when we walked in, excited to show us.

Either the cable was out, or there wasn't cable in the first place. But she had found two shelves of movies, and a VCR in the cupboard below the TV. She'd chosen *Gone With the Wind*. She told us she'd never seen it before, and was excited to watch it, because she knew it was a classic. She then proceeded to talk incessantly, missing out on the major plot points.

The adults gathered around the dining table, a pack of cards appearing, and settled in for an evening of euchre, and more drinking.

Dad set his cellphone down on the fireplace mantel, along with his pager from work. He must've forgotten to take it off before we left. Not surprising, since he wore it constantly. He caught me watching him and threw me a wink, wiggling his cellphone as he set it down. "This thing's useless out here. No signal." He clapped me on the back as he moved past me to join the others at the table.

The kids debated playing a card game ourselves, or one of the board games Katie had brought, but no one seemed to want to make a decision. I popped my hearing aids back on, clicking the battery doors shut. The world came back into focus again, the chatter from the grown-ups becoming suddenly loud in the small space.

In the end, Evelyn ended up with her book in her hand once again. She sat curled on the opposite end of the couch from me, stating absentmindedly that she would play whatever we all decided on, eyes glued to the page, already engrossed in what she was reading. Ryan made a stink about the movie, wanting to change it. He sat on the floor in front of the cabinet and looked through the titles two or three times, coming up with nothing good, apparently.

He flopped onto the loveseat. "There's nothing to do."

"Then choose a game already," Evelyn snapped. Ryan proceeded to sigh loudly, several times. I sat with my copy of *Dune*, closed in my lap. Evelyn eyed it and then looked up at me.

"Teddy, weren't you going to let Ryan read that?" She raised an eyebrow at me. I gave her a lopsided grin.

"Yeah, I forgot." I stood up and leaned over towards Ryan, extending the book out to him. "Here."

He looked at me for a moment, with an icy expression, before taking the book reluctantly from my hand.

I sank back down on the couch, looking at the TV for a moment or two. The volume was down low, too low for me to really follow what was being said. Katie had floated over to the adults and was watching the game. Gazing at their cards over their shoulders. It looked like they were explaining how it worked.

I sighed, and Evelyn's eyes flicked up to me. "Not you." She gave me a slightly disapproving look. I glanced down at the coffee table. The cheese and cracker tray had been cleared up. A thin paperback book lay on the table with a receipt sticking out of it. I tilted my head sideways trying to read the title, then reached out to pick it up.

"*Cryptids of Vermont,*" I read out loud, "*Local myths and legends.*"

Ryan's gaze landed on me. "My Dad bought that on the drive in. We stopped for a night in Burlington." He shook his head. "What a load of crap." He returned his gaze to *Dune*. It looked like he had read about two pages. I rolled my eyes and looked over at Evelyn, but she was lost in her book.

I flipped the cryptid book open and started to scan the pages. It was actually sort of interesting, or at least, entertaining. There was a chapter about Slipperyskin, an enormous bear-like creature that terrorized parts of Vermont in the 1700s. He got his name because he escaped from every trap that was set for him. There was also a chapter about the Glastenbury Wild Man. A little hand-drawn image showed a man running around half naked in the woods, with a wolf pelt draped over his head. I skimmed through that one for a few minutes.

I moved on to a chapter about Skin-walkers as the noise from the dining table rose. Apparently, the skin-walkers were a Navajo legend, notorious in the southwest. But there had been sightings locally here in Vermont, and in the Green Mountain National Forest specifically.

I tried to block out the chaos ensuing as the adults roared with another bout of laughter. Skin-walkers could take on the shape of any animal, or even a person, by wearing its skin, but it seemed that they could sometimes even use a person's hair to transform into them. You supposedly became a skin-walker by committing an evil act, typically by killing someone close to you, like a family member. I grimaced a little at that.

"What are you reading about Teddy?" I looked up to see Evelyn watching me closely. I shrugged.

"Skin-walkers. Apparently, the Green Mountain National Forest is riddled with them." She shook her head, grinning, while Ryan guffawed from the loveseat. I ignored him. "Listen to this: 'They are shape shifters, taking on the form of animals or even people, by wearing their skins. They are said to have supernatural abilities, like speed, mimicry, and even mind-control. The Navajo believed that they would appear white in color in their animal form, and this was the only way to distinguish them.'"

Ryan interjected, "Why would anyone believe that?"

Evelyn shrugged. "Things were different back then. Besides, they were like stories they told around the campfire, you know? It's not that much different from the books we write now; it's just telling stories."

I continued to skim the page, my eyes jumping ahead. "I guess they believed if you made eye contact with a skin-walker, your body would freeze up with fear. They can use your fear to gain power and energy. Saying their name out loud can attract them to you."

"Ooh, uh oh." Ryan had set Dune down on the love-seat next to him, not bothering to mark his spot. He wiggled his fingers at Evelyn, "Skin-walkers, skin-walkers, skin-walkers..." She pulled the throw pillow from behind her back and threw it at him. Ryan ducked, laughing.

"But get this, if you knew the true name of the skin-walker, you could say its full name out loud to it, and within three days, it would get sick and die." I shrugged. "Or, you can kill them by shooting them in the neck, with a bullet dipped in white ash..." I trailed off for a moment. "Hmm, interesting, it says they can't enter a dwelling without being invited in. Just like a vampire."

"Oh perfect." Ryan gestured to the door as he stood up. "Well, I'll just go dip all our bullets for tomorrow in white ash, you know, just in case." He rolled his eyes and picked up the throw pillow, chucking it at my face. The book was knocked out of my hands onto the floor. "I'm grabbing a soda, does anyone want one?"

"I'll take a Vernors," I said.

"Vernors?" Ryan sneered. "What the heck is that?"

"It's the green cans." I jerked a thumb towards the kitchen. Ryan shrugged and shuffled past me. He made it to the end of the couch when he cried out and jumped back a step, knocking into my knee. I whipped my head around.

"What the fuck?" he murmured.

"Ryan!" Sandy looked over at him, mouth slightly agape. "Language!" The adults had grown suddenly quiet. Dave snorted a bit, covering his mouth with his hand as Sandy shot him a look.

"I saw someone watching us," Ryan exclaimed, arms held out at his sides. "Staring through the window." He pointed then to the small window above their heads. Everyone swiveled to look at the window, set high in the wall. Only the dark sky was visible through the glass. "I swear," Ryan said, "there was a face, it..." his voice trailed off.

Bang-bang-bang, a knock sounded suddenly at the door. Mrs. Michelle let out a little yelp, grabbing onto Mrs. Sandy's arm. They dissolved in a fit of giggles. "There's someone knocking at the door, that's all," Mrs. Sandy chuckled.

"I got it." Ryan's dad stood up and made his way over to the door. I watched my dad; he was looking up at the window, then back at the door, his back stiff.

I heard voices at the front door and turned to face the other way. Dr. Carter was ushering in two people. "Please, come in, man it got cold out there." An older couple stepped into the entryway.

The man was freakishly tall; he had to stoop to fit through the door frame. His head crowned in a mop of white hair, face framed in a long grey and white beard. The woman next to him wore her long hair in two thick braids, trailing almost down to the belt tying her coat closed at her waist. She carried a large platter covered in tin foil in both arms.

"Nice to see you all folks, I hope you're having a pleasant evening." There were murmurs of acquiescence all around. "We wanted to stop by earlier, apologies for the late visit."

Nonsense." Dr. Carter looked at his watch. "it's only seven, not late at all."

"Well, we ended up spending far too much time in town, more than we'd planned. We like to be here to greet guests in the afternoon." He gestured towards the tray. "Mrs. Johnson made you some chocolate chip cookies, as a little welcome gift." She beamed and held out the tray towards Ryan's dad. Dr. Carter grabbed it from her, carrying it over to the dining table. Mrs. Montgomery stood up and made her way around the table.

"Thank you, that is so kind of you." She held her hand out to the woman. "I'm Michelle, so nice to meet you in person." They shook hands. "Everything has been perfect so far, by the way, exactly what we hoped for."

"Oh." Mrs. Johnson turned to smile up at the man I presumed was Mr. Johnson. "We're so glad to hear that dear, I can't tell you how happy that makes us. Why, I was just saying the other day, we hadn't had a renter in so long," she chuckled nervously, "that I was starting to think there was something wrong." She clasped her hands together. "I worry, you know? I started thinking maybe there was a problem with the property. Maybe folks weren't finding it to their liking."

"No, not at all." Mrs. Michelle shook her head. "I think it will suit us nicely for the weekend, we're very pleased so far."

"Well." Mrs. Johnson moved over to the table and began to remove the tin foil from the large tray. "And of course, after what happened to that poor girl, we didn't think we'd have anyone come to stay for quite some time." She shook her head sadly. "Please, have a cookie." She held the tray out towards Dad and Dr. M.

Dr. Montgomery reached forward, grabbing a cookie, his eyes still on Mrs. Johnson. Dad just watched her wearily. "What poor girl?" Katie's voice squeaked. She stood behind her mom's chair, both hands gripped around the spinnerets at the top, watching Mrs. Johnson.

Mrs. Johnson shook her head. "Oh, that... it was a terrible business. Young girl here with her family for a long holiday weekend. Such a nice family. Beautiful family." She shook her head again, sighing. "Apparently, she snuck out at night, though lord knows where she thought she was going out here, in the middle of nowhere. Maybe she was planning on meeting someone." She shook her head again. "The police spent days searching. It was all over the news. Not the sort of publicity you want, is it?"

I looked over at Mr. Johnson. He still stood by the doorway, next to Ryan's dad. His posture was casual, shoulders rounded and arms slack. He appeared relaxed, but his eyes roved around the room, flickering over each face, as though he were studying us one by one. Was he watching our reactions to the story?

"That's terrible," Mrs. Michelle murmured. "We didn't hear anything about it. Was this recently?"

"She stayed here?" Katie gulped, eyes wide. "What happened to her?"

"They never found her, dummy." Ryan rolled his eyes, folding his arms across his chest. Mr. Johnson's attention flickered in his direction.

"Ryan," Mrs. Sandy murmured, giving him a look.

"Oh no, they found her all right." Mrs. Johnson shook her head. "They found her in pieces, out in those woods. And it wasn't just her, either. Oh no..." she cleared her throat, "They found too many body parts for it to have been one person." She gestured towards the back of the house with her chin. A thick silence fell.

"Cookie?" She held the tray out towards Mrs. Sandy and Katie. Katie's eyes were like saucers.

"Jesus," Mrs. Sandy muttered. She grimaced down at the cookies. "No, thank you."

"Well," Mrs. Johnson sighed, setting the tray back down on the table. "Nothing like that's happened since, thank the lord."

Mr. Johnson spoke up suddenly, his deep voice reverberating in the small space. "That's right. Probably some hitchhikers, teenagers, or someone passing through, got up to no good. There hasn't been an issue since. Course, it's best not to go out in those woods alone at night. Anyone local would know better than that." He chuckled as though there was something funny about it. Then he clapped his hands together loudly. "Well, we best be going, Mrs. Johnson, don't want to take up too much of your evening, folks." He held his hand up and Mrs. Johnson moved back to join him at the door.

"Yes, have a pleasant evening, and you know where to find us should you need anything at all during your stay. We're just the first house after the turn." She pointed as they moved out the door. "Just up the road."

"Why would anyone local know better?" I heard myself ask out loud.

Mr. Johnson paused, hand already grasping the handle. He turned back to find me, dark eyes meeting mine. "Well..." he trailed off for a second, stroking his beard with one hand, he glanced at his wife. "What's your name, son?"

"Teddy," I murmured.

"Well, Teddy, the locals know better because this place has a history. Going back as early as the 1700s, there have been stories. Stories about the woods, the wilderness up near Glastenbury. And not just that, there have been other... disappearances." There was a pregnant pause, and no one spoke for several seconds. Mr. Johnson turned away from the door, taking a step back into the room. "There are records of disappearances going back to the early 1900s. People who've strayed alone, up in those woods, especially at night, or around dusk, they don't come back. Never seen, never heard from again. That's as typically is the case. Although, there have been some instances, like this poor girl, where... evidence, is found, after the fact." Mrs. Johnson was watching us; watching our faces in turn, as he spoke. Was that a look of sorrow in her eyes? Or was it something else?

"So that's why I say, the locals, they'd know better. You won't catch anyone local anywhere near the woods at night. And certainly not alone." He gave me a look then, like he was warning me. Like he thought I had a secret hankering to go for a little midnight hike, all by my lonesome. He turned slightly, as if he was about to leave, but turned back again.

"None of you wear a red coat, do you?" He scanned our faces, as we shook our heads one by one. Furrowed brows and confused frowns. "Well, that's just as well then. It's considered bad luck to wear red, out in these woods." He waved a hand and laughed. "Just a local superstition. A few who went missing happened to wear red coats: Paula Weldon, and that Jepson boy..." he trailed off again, his dark eyes growing cold. He waved a hand. "But that's all it is, just superstition." He met my eyes again briefly, and there was no warmth, no glint of humor in them. Then he turned. "You folks take care now. Have a good night."

We murmured goodnight and waved as they exited and pulled the door shut behind them. We were quiet for a moment. "Well, that was weird," Evelyn murmured from her chair. She stared at the closed door.

Ryan blew out a breath and grinned, chuckling a little. "Sounds like your skin-walkers must have got them, Teddy." He stooped and picked up the book, tossing it at me. I held up the throw pillow to block it and it fell onto the couch at my side, but when he wasn't looking, I picked it up, staring down at the cover for a moment. I flipped it open again and paged through to the next chapter. Were the people he mentioned in here? The ones who went missing?

Ryan's dad peered over the couch at the book. "Oh yeah, I was flipping through there the other night. He's right; there are a lot of local legends about creatures out in the woods. Who would have thought, in Vermont?" He chuckled for a moment, then his expression turned dark. "But no, Ry," he cleared his throat, reaching up with his right index finger, he pressed the bridge of his glasses up. "That story didn't sound like it had anything to do with a creature. Sometimes, people can be the worst monsters."

"David," Sandy exclaimed, her tone reproachful. "That's enough of that, thank you very much." She turned to look at Katie, grabbing her hand and leading her over towards the seating area. "Why don't you kids play a game, hmm? Where's that bag of board games we brought?"

4

— • —

We spent the remainder of the evening playing *Monopoly* at Katie's insistence. I groaned a little when she selected it, knowing it was one of those games that could take hours.

The adults slowly got drunker, our dads taking turns telling old stories from med school, as we sipped our pop and bought properties. I eyed the chocolate chip cookies more than once, but for some reason I didn't really want to eat one.

Eventually, the adults got tired. They decided to call it a night around ten or so. Our game was finally about to wind up. Katie had already dropped out, ironically, but Ryan refused to quit, and I wasn't about to let him win.

Katie walked home with her mom and dad, one arm through Mrs. Sandy's, and Ryan called out that he would head back as soon as we finished.

Dad headed downstairs to his room, reminding me not to stay up too late. Dr. M and Mrs. Michelle went downstairs to their room too, Mrs. M waving a hand at the kitchen, saying they'd tidy up tomorrow. She swayed slightly on her feet, and Dr. M held a hand out to steady her. Evelyn rolled her eyes at me as they traipsed down the stairs, but she was grinning.

It was late, and our game was starting to get old. I was losing interest, but I tried to stay focused on beating Ryan. He got distracted and started chatting up Evelyn about his winning football season. I tried to roll my eyes at her, but she didn't seem to notice me. I sighed and got up, carrying my empty can of Vernors with me.

"Where are you going Teddy?" Evelyn called out after me.

I held up the can over my shoulder, "Just going to throw this in the recycling, be right back."

I headed over to the front door, pausing, remembering I didn't have my shoes on. I found them in the dark in the pile of shoes by the closet and shoved my feet into them without bothering to pull them on all the way or untie them, my ankles hanging off the back.

I opened the front door and looked out. It was pitch black out there. There were no streetlamps on this stretch of dirt road, but I knew there was a light over to the left of the door, above the garage, that was motion sensored. We'd set it off earlier when we returned from target shooting, it had been just dark enough. I stepped onto the porch, waving my arms to try to trigger it, but it wouldn't turn on. I knew the recycling bin was somewhere over on the side of the house, but I wasn't sure I wanted to wander around in the dark to try to find it. Not to mention it was freezing out.

I stepped back inside, closing the door behind me, and ducked into the kitchen instead, setting the can next to the sink. I felt a tiny sliver of shame at being afraid of the dark.

I moved to the kitchen doorway and heard Evelyn's voice, pitched low. "Oh, come on Ryan, that's ridiculous."

"Is it?" he murmured back. "Did you see him earlier? Did you see the look on his face after? He was eying me like I was his next target."

"Ryan..." Evelyn began. I froze in the doorway, listening.

"You gotta admit he's a little weird, Evelyn. He's like the weird quiet kid that brings a gun to school out of nowhere."

"Stop it," she hissed. "He would never hurt anyone. You don't know what you're talking about."

"Oh yeah? You sure about that?" Silence. No response from Evelyn. "Don't tell me you actually like him?" Ryan snorted, an edge of emotion to his voice. "He's a freak." My heart pounded in my chest.

"Why? Because he's different? Because of his hearing aids? Why would you say that, Ryan? Grow up." Evelyn's voice rose louder now. I felt my hands clenching into fists, my jaw tightening.

Ryan spat back at her, "It's not just that. Come on Ev, you saw him earlier, he started freaking out for no reason. He does that all the time! Don't you remember when we were kids? He just... lashes out, like he can't control himself."

"He gets overwhelmed sometimes, it's not..." she trailed off, her voice uncertain now. "He would never hurt anyone..."

"Yeah, you willing to bet on that?" Ryan murmured. "Because I'm not." His voice sank lower as he continued. I strained to try to hear Evelyn's response back, but they were speaking too quietly now, and I was too far away. I felt my eyes starting to burn slightly. I moved a step closer, then another, straining to make out what they were saying. The fact that they were sitting there, talking about me like that, about what a freak I was... the uncertainty in Evelyn's voice. It was like a knife in my chest.

Evelyn's head whipped to the side, and she stared up at me with wide eyes. "Oh, Teddy..." she trailed off. She stood, moving a step towards me, "Teddy... listen-"

I cut her off. "Forget about it," I replied, my voice clipped. I gestured to the gameboard spread out on the coffee table. "I'm done with this. I'm going to bed." Ryan didn't move, staring up at me from his seat on the floor, legs tucked under the coffee table. He leaned back casually, propping himself up against the loveseat behind him.

I refused to look at him, refused to meet his eyes. Good to know for sure what he thought about me. I couldn't say I was surprised.

Evelyn opened her mouth, about to say something further, but seemed to think better of it. She began to clear up the game, stacking the paper money in the box. Ryan helped her. I sat on the armchair, watching them. They cleared up the gameboard quickly and Ryan got to his feet, stretching and groaning.

"Well, I'm heading back. Have a good night, guys." He had the decency to sound uncomfortable at least, but I still wouldn't look at him. He moved to the doorway and slipped on his shoes and grabbed his coat from the closet. I said nothing, sitting in silence with my chin in my hands.

"Goodnight," Evelyn called to him glumly. He moved to the doorway, catching my eye finally and winking at me, his right eye shuttering briefly, just before he disappeared into the darkness, swinging the door shut behind him.

I insisted to Evelyn that I didn't need help setting up the pull-out couch, refusing to make eye contact. She finally gave up and headed upstairs. I was to sleep in the family room because there weren't any other bedrooms available. Evelyn was taking the futon upstairs in the loft.

She lingered for another few seconds at the bottom of the stairs as though she was going to say something, but then she whispered goodnight to me, and made her way up the stairs.

I murmured a gruff and garbled goodnight back to her and dragged the coffee table out of the way, moving it over in front of the French glass doors.

I removed the couch cushions and threw them against the wall, pulling the metal bed frame out and unfolding it. Thankfully it was already made up with sheets at least. Rooting around in the closet, I found a thick comforter. I threw that over the bed and used one of the throw pillows propped up on a couch cushion as my pillow.

After I'd been laying there for several minutes, I realized I'd forgotten to take my hearing aids out. I got up with a groan and pulled them off, clicking the battery doors open and setting them in my case from my bag. I grabbed my toothbrush too and ducked into the bathroom to brush my teeth.

I lay there for a long time afterward in the dark, arms folded behind my head, eyes straying to the half wall of the loft above me, and the darkness beyond.

I thought of Evelyn, lying up there, and wondered if she was still awake too, so close to me, but out of reach. I thought about climbing the stairs in the dark, climbing onto the bed beside her, taking her in my arms. I pictured her wrapping her arms around me, hands sliding behind my neck, pulling me to her. Her lips on mine. Yeah right. She'd probably just scream.

I sighed loudly, flipping over onto my side to stare out the glass doors, over the balcony, the crown of the woods surrounding us just barely visible against the dark night sky.

I noticed the cryptid book, still lying on the coffee table, and grabbed it. I sat for a while in the armchair, back to the window, using the pale moonlight streaming in to read by.

There was quite a bit about the disappearances, a whole chapter dedicated to them, actually. The saddest one was the little boy: the Jepson boy, that Mr. Johnson had mentioned. I hated anything like that, anything to do with little kids. I thought of him wandering alone out in the woods, scared, and it made me feel sick.

I gave up reading after that, tossing the book back onto the coffee table, and forced myself to try to sleep again. I struggled to get comfortable on the old creaky pullout bed. I could feel metal bars through the mattress, digging into my back. My stomach churned slightly as I thought of the Jepson boy, of twisted shadows, monsters lurking out in the woods, shadows beneath the trees morphing into crooked claws and jagged teeth. And the thought kept nagging at me, in the back of my mind, as my eyes finally grew heavy: there hadn't been any mention of him wearing red in the book.

I must have drifted off eventually, because I woke some unknown amount of time later, my eyes straining to adjust as I propped myself up on one elbow.

"Teddy..." I heard a hoarse voice calling out to my left, from over near the armchair. "Teddy, wake up!"

"Jesus, Ev? What's going on?" I whispered back to her as my eyes finally adjusted to the dark, making out her staring back at me, eyes so wide I could see the whites all around them, practically glowing in the moonlight.

"I heard something. There's someone out there. Outside the house." I moved to a seated position, swinging my legs over the edge of the bed and immediately hitting my ankle on a metal bar.

"Ouch," I murmured. "Maybe it's an animal you heard? A deer or something, moving around?"

Evelyn shook her head. She moved closer to me, on her knees next to me, she leaned onto the bed. "No, Teddy, they were... knocking. Like on purpose." She kept her voice pitched low, and she kept turning to look out the French glass doors, and the window over the dining table. Head swiveling back and forth.

"Knocking? Like on the door?" I turned to look over at the front door, squinting in the dark.

"I don't think so. It didn't sound like it was on the door. It sounded like they were knocking on the walls, moving around the house. But there's more than one, I think."

"What's the point of that? What are they trying to do?"

"Scare us, I guess?" She shrugged, "I really don't know. And I don't think we want to find out."

I stood up but she grabbed my arm, pulling me back down. I slammed back onto the edge of the bed. "Don't Teddy." She hissed at me. "I'm scared. We don't know who's out there."

"I was just going to look out the window, see if I could see anything." I shook my head at her. She still had a grip on my arm, her nails digging into my forearm. "It's probably just someone messing around." I looked back towards the front door again. The guns were out in the car. Dad and I had locked them back up in the trunk after we were done target shooting.

I heard it then, a low dull, *bang-bang-bang*. The cadence was slow and deliberate. We both froze, Evelyn gripped my arm tighter. "See," she hissed. She stared over at the front door. The knocking sound had definitely come from the front of the house.

We sat in silence for a moment. Then it came again, Evelyn's head whipping to the side. This time it was off to her right, the far wall, over by the dining table. I stood up, and she tried to pull me back at first, then rose with me this time.

She stood so close to me, I could smell a faint scent, like vanilla and peaches. I turned to her and laid my hand on top of hers. I felt the death-grip on my arm lessen slightly. "I'm just going to peek out the window, it's okay."

Her wide eyes didn't leave mine, strands of her hair falling around her face in loose messy curls that had escaped from the bun piled on top of her head. She nodded solemnly once, and let go of my bicep, hands sliding down my arm. I moved to the window. My heart banging in my chest had nothing to do with whatever was outside.

I peered through the corner of the window; I was just tall enough on tiptoes to see out. It was dark enough now that I could hardly make out the tree line, but I saw what appeared to be an empty swath of ground below the window. Nothing visible. I waited a minute or so, but nothing moved. "Maybe it was the wind," I called over to her. "Knocking something against the house."

Light flooded my view suddenly, and it took me a moment to figure out what had happened. The motion sensor light over the garage had been triggered. There was something moving out there after all.

I moved swiftly to the kitchen doorway, making my way over to the window above the sink. It overlooked the front of the house. I propped myself up on the edge of the sink, straining to see the driveway leading up to the garage.

A pool of light flooded the driveway, but I could see nothing moving out there. "Teddy," Evelyn hissed at me from the kitchen doorway.

I turned to her, "I don't see anything. The light came on though. There was definitely something moving around out there."

Evelyn nodded at me, then moved cautiously over to the sink. I shifted over and she leaned over the sink as well, peering out the window.

"*Hawoooo, oww oww awhoooo.*" A howl loosed into the night from somewhere in the immediate vicinity. It was coyote-like, but had an eerie, mournful quality to it. Evelyn jumped back, away from the sink.

"A wolf?" She turned to me and whispered breathlessly, eyes wide.

I shook my head. "Maybe. But it sounded more like a coyote to me."

She stared at me. "How could it make a knocking sound like that?"

I stared back at her a moment before shaking my head wordlessly.

"I'm going out there to look," I said, moving past her.

"Teddy don't." She reached for me, but I was already moving.

"I'm just going to take a look," I insisted, but she shook her head, angling in front of me and pressing her back to the front door. "Ev," I breathed. "It's just someone messing with us."

"Then let them!" she exclaimed in a hoarse whisper. She put her hand on my chest. "You are not going out there alone; I'll go get–"

The knocking started then. It came from all around us. The back of the house, the front, from both sides. The walls practically rattled. It was like there was a whole group of people out there, banging on the walls at the same time. Evelyn's eyes went wide.

The banging surrounded us, increasing in intensity. Evelyn grabbed me, hand gripped around my bicep. She shrank into me, against my chest. I could barely hear her over the knocking.

"What's happening?" She peered up at me, eyes wide in fear. I wrapped an arm around her, and moved her away from the door, into the main room of the house.

"Come on," I yelled to her over the clattering. I took her hand, and led her down the stairs, to where our parents slept. I couldn't imagine how anyone could sleep through this racket, and while it was noticeably quieter downstairs, the knocking was definitely still audible down here, even to me.

Dad's door slammed open into the hallway just as we reached the bottom of the stairs. "What the hell is going on?" He called over to me, eyes wide, grey hair mussed with sleep.

I shook my head. "There's someone out there, messing around. They were knocking on the walls, in different spots, but now it's all over like they're surrounding the house. We heard..." my voice was suddenly too loud in the silence as the knocking stopped abruptly. "A coyote out there, too." I added, at a now more appropriate volume.

"Okay." Dad nodded, laying a hand on my shoulder, nodding. "We'll check it out. See what's going on." As he spoke, the door down the hall creaked open, and Dr. M poked his head out into the hallway.

"What the heck is going on out there?" he asked, squinting at us, his voice thick and angry.

"There's someone out there," Evelyn squeaked from behind my shoulder. "They were banging on the walls, all at once." Dr. M frowned over at her, taking in her hand still gripped in mine. I let go abruptly.

"Let's go check it out Jim," Dad murmured to Dr. M. "Of course, the dang guns are out in the car." He disappeared back into the bedroom for a moment and returned with his jeans on, shrugging into a fleece jacket.

Dr. M ducked back into the room to change too, and returned a minute or so later. Mrs. Michelle didn't emerge from the bedroom, and he clicked the door shut behind him.

They led the way back upstairs, Evelyn and I trailed behind them. Dad flicked the lights on. Evelyn stood in the family room, arms tucked tight around her, still in her oversized sweatshirt, shaking her head back and forth wordlessly as I slipped my shoes on.

Dad and Dr. M moved outside onto the front porch, and I looked back at her. She glared at me disapprovingly. "It'll be okay, I'll be right back." She shook her head again and sighed, turning away from me to stare out the French glass doors.

I stepped out into the cold, pulling the door shut behind me. I followed as they moved down the few steps to the gravel walkway and headed for the driveway. There was nothing in front of the garage, but the light was still on. Dad headed straight for our car, the headlights flashed, and he must have hit the button on the key fob repeatedly, because the horn honked, the piercing sound causing me to jump. Well, whoever was out here knew we were here now, there was no doubt about that.

He moved to the trunk. I moved behind him, around to where I could get a view of the side of the house, not venturing further, but hanging back so I could keep an eye on Dad. He had unlocked the gun safe and pulled out the shiny black handgun. He grabbed my shotgun, and looked over at me, eyebrows raised as he held it out in my direction.

I paused for a second then moved over to take it, gripping the barrel, but he didn't let go, meeting my eyes. "This isn't permission to shoot anything that moves, Ted. Don't get trigger happy." I met his stare and nodded solemnly. He let go of the gun.

He grabbed one of the other shotguns and handed it to Dr. M, then pulled a handful of shells out of the box and passed them around quickly.

We did a full sweep of the perimeter of the house, then moved a few feet into the woods, scanning the property the best we could in the dark. We didn't find anyone, person or animal.

I searched the ground below the dining room window. There were some possible footprints, boot prints, potentially, in the mud below the window, but Ryan had seen someone, probably Mr. Johnson, peeking in through the window earlier. Those tracks were easily explained.

I found a scuff mark in the mud here or there, but no clear trail I could follow. Behind the house, out in the small backyard, right near the entrance to the little trail that led back to the clearing, I found a clearer track in a patch of mud where the grass had been worn down.

Whatever it was, it was long, more like a human footprint than anything else, definitely not from a wolf or coyote, not from a deer. It didn't appear to be from a shoe or a boot, either. It almost looked like it was made by someone walking barefoot, but the print looked oddly elongated. And why would anyone be walking out here barefoot at night? I shrugged and moved on. The print didn't lead anywhere besides the trail, and I moved a few feet down it and didn't come across more.

We gave up and headed back to the front porch. Dad looked back at the car, and I saw him thinking about putting the guns back for the night, but he and Dr. M murmured something to each other, and we headed back inside, taking them with us.

Evelyn's face flooded with relief when she saw us reenter the house. Dad insisted we set the guns next to the front door. We double checked it was locked, and he made sure the French glass doors were locked, as well as the backdoor that was downstairs, which led out into the backyard.

They sent Evelyn back upstairs to bed, and Dad told me to lie down and try to get some sleep. He seemed somewhat reluctant to leave me upstairs, but it was just as safe as anywhere else in the house. Besides, I told myself, nothing had happened in the end.

But as I lay there, I thought of that knocking, being everywhere all at once, surrounding us. It took much longer for me to drift off to sleep this time.

5

— • —

My breath plumed in clouds of white, rising and disappearing into the air. Evelyn sat to my left, her back to me, both of us leaning against either side of the fallen tree we had chosen. Dad had the large deer blind and was sharing it with Dr. M. They were about a half mile or so off to our left. Dr. Carter was another quarter mile or so beyond them.

Dr. Montgomery had staked out the area yesterday before we'd arrived, dragging Evelyn and Mrs. Michelle along with him. He'd scoped the place out online before the trip, and had a pretty good idea of where he wanted to set up. They had been lucky and found what looked like a deer run fairly quickly, and had set up the blinds nearby.

As soon as we'd parked, Dad had spread out the map of the Green Mountain National Forest that he'd brought on the hood of our car. He showed us where we were on the map: in an area marked '*The Glastenbury Wilderness*'. Trail #326 lay to the northeast, and Mount Snow just a few miles beyond that, the ski runs visible on the map. There wasn't much else in the general vicinity.

The area between our location and trail #326 was labeled *Somerset*. I recalled Dad had pointed that out to me earlier, before we left. He said it was a tiny, old town; the current population now was down to 6. There were no local roads in our immediate vicinity according to the map, other than the one we'd taken in.

"What's this?" I asked, pointing to an area to the west of our location. There were several buildings marked on the map, in the middle of nowhere.

"Oh that," Dr. Carter said, speaking up from over my shoulder. "That's the old town of Glastenbury. Abandoned. Around there was where the Bennington Monster was sighted. Did you get to that part in the book last night?" I turned to look at him, shaking my head.

"There were some folks attacked by an 8-foot tall, hairy monster in these parts. Some think it may have been a yeti that they saw, but others think it was actually the Glastenbury Wild Man."

He paused, pushing his glasses back up with his index finger. "They ran him out of town, and he ended up living out in the woods alone. They said he turned cannibalistic, went insane. He could be sighted running around in animal furs, attacking settlers traveling through the mountains. The town was already well on the decline, at that point, too remote, too isolated, up in the mountains. There's an old hotel up there, and what used to be a casino. The last residents of the town were a family of three."

He nodded, looking off into the distance. "The Native Americans thought Glastenbury mountain was haunted actually, or cursed. They refused to go there. Other than to bury their dead, apparently. There's an old graveyard up here somewhere as well that the settlers used." I nodded thoughtfully, eyeing the map again.

"Don't get any ideas," Dad said, marking our cars on the map with a pencil stub. We'd taken two cars, our SUV and Dr. M's truck, to drive out here. Dr. Carter had left his car, a black Lincoln, with Mrs. Michelle and Mrs. Sandy.

He'd handed his wife the keys before we left, making a joke about her getting another parking ticket in Burlington. She'd laughed, blushed a little, and swiped the keys from his outstretched hand before slapping him on the arm. He'd laughed in response, reaching up with his right index finger and pushing his glasses back up on the bridge of his nose. I didn't know why he always did that. It almost looked like he was flicking everyone off. And his glasses never seemed to actually be actually sliding down his nose. It seemed like more of a nervous habit than anything else.

Dad folded up the map carefully, making sure to fold it back in exactly the same way it had been before. "It's not safe to go exploring in old, abandoned buildings like that. Not to mention it's illegal." He'd brought his old compass with him, like always. He handed both the folded map and the compass to me when he was done. "Keep these safe, Teddy."

I mumbled something back, shoving the map and compass into my inner coat pocket. They'd woken us up at an ungodly early hour, and I was still groggy. But we needed to be out and in place well before sunrise to have any chance of bagging a deer.

Dad and Dr. M were banging around the kitchen by 4:30, seemingly unaffected by either the number of beers they had consumed, or the time spent searching outside the house last night. Although I noted massive amounts of coffee had been made and drank before we even made it to the trailhead.

Dr. Carter was another story. He had stumbled through the front door, complaining of a headache, with Katie close behind him, complaining loudly that it was too early to be up. Ryan must have been lagging behind. His dad waved him angrily through the door. "What are you lollygagging around for? Get in."

Dr. C rolled his eyes at Dad, behind Ryan's back. "Coffee," he murmured, clearly scenting the fresh brew in the air. Dad held up a finger and went into the kitchen to get him some. Dr. Carter had sighed in relief as he took the outstretched mug. Ryan greeted us with a quick smile and a nod to the room in general, looking oddly refreshed and perky for 4:30 in the morning.

He gave no indication that he felt any remorse over what I'd overheard him saying last night. *Shocker.* But he did make an effort to help with breakfast and even went so far as to offer me a steaming cup of coffee.

I'd declined it, although I'd almost said yes, out of shock. I wasn't a coffee drinker. Evelyn was though, apparently. She had taken the cup Ryan held out to her gratefully, still wiping sleep from her eyes.

Ryan had frowned a little at my tone of voice when I'd said no; I'd spoken a bit sharply. "Is everything okay, Teddy?" He'd asked me, brows wrinkling slightly.

"Oh, yeah. Everything's just great, Ryan," I'd said sarcastically back to him.

"Really? Because you seem a little... irritated, this morning." I stared at him for a moment in confusion. His expression was honest-looking, open, like he was being serious. But then he gave me a lopsided grin, and I knew he was just messing with me again.

I pitched my voice lower, glancing over at Evelyn. She was reading her book. "Gee, I dunno, Ryan. Maybe it's the fact that you were telling Evelyn I'm some kind of psychopath, who would bring a gun to school," I snapped. "I dunno man, if I thought that about someone... I think I might make more of an effort not to be a total dick to them."

He frowned for a second, eyes flickering back and forth over mine as I glared at him. Then he just shrugged, snorting a little. "Whatever man. You're too sensitive." He rolled his eyes and continued on his way, moving on to offer the mug to Evelyn.

When he'd returned to the kitchen, she sipped it, quiet for a moment or so. Then she set her book down, and turned to me and said abruptly. "What was that last night? I still don't get what happened."

I stared blankly back at her, still not fully awake myself. It took me a moment to figure out what she was talking about, my mind still on Ryan. "Oh, I... I don't know, Ev. I really don't know." I thought for a moment. "The howl we heard did sound like a coyote though. I've heard them before, up at my grandpa's property up north. But the knocking..." I trailed off, at a loss for any theories to propose.

Evelyn didn't respond, and I followed her gaze to the coffee table, still pushed over in front of the glass door wall. She appeared to be staring at the cryptid book.

Dad had clapped his hands suddenly from a few feet away, drawing our attention. "Time to get packed up to head out, kids." Evelyn groaned loudly. She complained about not having time to drink her coffee, until Dr. M produced disposable travel mugs Mrs. Michelle had packed. She poured her coffee in reluctantly and went for a warmup.

She still sipped from it, slowly, from her seat behind me, cupping it in her gloved hands. It must have retained enough heat to provide her with some additional warmth. I thought with longing of the hand warmers that Mom would have thought to pack for us, had she come on the trip.

We were up early enough that the air still held a bite of cold, but I hoped it would dissipate eventually, once the sun came up fully. It wasn't very chilly yesterday, but I knew weather patterns worked differently up in the mountains, and we were at a higher elevation here, though not in the mountains proper.

I kept my eyes peeled for deer, for any movement amongst the thick foliage that surrounded us. There were still enough leaves on the trees to provide good coverage and camouflage. We had chosen a spot near a small clearing. I had a decent line of sight through the trees into the clearing. The sun should be starting to rise in the next half hour or so, but for now, the forest remained drenched in darkness.

Ryan and Katie were posted up about two hundred yards off to our right. Although I couldn't make out her words, I heard Katie's voice every now and then as she chattered on to Ryan. I winced slightly every time. She had to be talking loudly for me to hear her from this far away. Evelyn chuckled slightly next to my ear as Katie's voice drifted over to us once again.

"She's going to scare all the deer away," Evelyn murmured to me. "I'm sure Ryan is just thrilled right now."

I grinned slightly and nodded. "Honestly, fine by me. Although it will make for a boring morning."

"A cold, boring morning," Evelyn corrected as she stretched her legs and made an exaggerated shivering motion. I turned to watch her. Her cheeks and the end of her nose were flushed pink from the cold. She pulled her scarf up and tucked her face into it. "Mmmhmmm mmm mmm." Was all I could gather.

"What?" I asked her, watching her eyes as though they'd give me some kind of hint. I had my earmuffs slung around my neck. Dad always made me promise to wear them if I took a shot. The reality was, there likely wouldn't be time to slip them on if I did get a chance and I obviously couldn't hear anything coming with them on. I wore them around my neck and that seemed to be enough of a compromise.

Evelyn tugged her scarf down. "Sorry," she murmured, "I was saying, I don't know how much longer I can stand sitting out here. I can't imagine Katie will last too much longer."

I sighed and nodded, eyebrows raised. "Well, that's going to be a problem. I guess if she can't stick it out, we can head over and let our dads know. I know they won't want to quit though. Maybe she can fit in the deer blind with them and warm up a little at least." I sighed again. "They'd probably just make us take her back to the cars. There's nowhere else to go."

Evelyn nodded, sighing as well. "She should have just stayed with Mom and Mrs. Sandy. Spending the day shopping in Burlington seems like it would have been right up her alley."

"I know." I peered back out towards the clearing, trying to stay focused. "I was surprised honestly that she didn't change her mind at the last minute." Evelyn nodded, taking another small sip of her coffee.

I pulled my gaze away from her and focused back on the tree line up ahead; still a whole lot of nothing. Then I paused. I thought I had caught a flash of movement, off to the right of the clearing. I peered at the spot, but could see nothing out of the ordinary, just the familiar bends and twists of tree branches, the gentle swaying of pine boughs in the wind.

"Teddy, about last night..." Evelyn was still talking, her voice pitched low, mindful of the need to be quiet. I tried to focus on her words, but there it was again. A flash of something, moving too quickly, independent of the wind. But what was it? I couldn't make out four legs, or even two, and it seemed to me that the movement had been high up. Too high for a deer.

"Teddy, are you listening?" Evelyn sighed, turning to me, and placing a hand on my arm. I brought my shotgun up, laying it across my lap.

"Mhmm," I murmured, keeping still, alert. Although I didn't see anything. No further movement now. Maybe it was just a bird. Or a squirrel.

"I said, I really need to talk to you about last night."

I grabbed her arm, still draped over the fallen log, and squeezed it gently. I felt her still. "Evelyn," I whispered, "quiet." I nodded forward, indicating the direction with my head, "I think there's something there."

She froze and stared in the direction I had been homed in on. Two sets of eyes were better than one, but we stayed that way, frozen in place, for several seconds, and nothing happened.

"A deer?" she murmured eventually. "I can't see it."

I shook my head. "I'm not sure what it is. It seemed too tall, too high up to be a deer. Almost like–"

Katie screamed suddenly, and both Evelyn and I jumped. The scream trailed off and was followed by a crashing sound. Footsteps, running through the underbrush. Evelyn managed to get to her feet first and started running in their direction.

I followed close behind her, turning once as I ran to look back towards the clearing. I came to a stumbling halt, staring. I thought I could make out a tall figure, shrouded in darkness on the edge of the clearing. Pale limbs and a stooping, almost bowed silhouette. Katie screamed again, and I turned away, running harder to catch up to Evelyn. Whatever it was causing Katie to scream like that, I didn't want Evelyn to encounter it first.

"Evelyn!" I called out to her, and she slowed, peering at me over her shoulder. "Wait up," I called out again. She slowed further and paused, waiting for me. I reached her and said "Thanks." She nodded, panting slightly, and fell in beside me. We took off again at a light jog.

Katie and Ryan burst through a patch of evergreens up ahead, about ten yards away. Katie was running ahead, with Ryan trailing behind.

"Teddy!" She slowed when she spotted us and burst into tears. Ryan came to a stop just behind her, barely avoiding running into her. He was slightly out of breath, panting as he leaned forward, putting his hands on his knees. He shook his head and looked up at us as we jogged over. Evelyn reached Katie first and tucked an arm around her.

"You idiot," Ryan said, "there goes any chance we had of getting a deer today. You probably screamed loud enough to scare them away for miles around." He continued shaking his head, a look of disgust on his face.

"Who cares about the stupid deer?" Katie shrieked, wheeling around to glare at him. "What on earth was that, Ryan?" He just continued to shake his head, standing upright now, hands on his hips. "What was that?" Katie shrieked again, staring at him, demanding an answer.

"I don't know what you're talking about Katie, I didn't see anything!" He held his arms out, yelling back at her now.

"Hey," Evelyn said, holding her hands up, moving between them. "Let's just calm down. What happened Katie?" Evelyn watched Katie, waiting for a response, but she just stared at Ryan, mouth gaped open, shaking her head. Evelyn reached out and rubbed her back in circles, as Katie's chest rose and fell rapidly.

"I saw something, in the trees up ahead of us," Katie gasped. "It was watching us," she continued, "It was... it was..." she trailed off. "I don't know what the heck it was. It was like a person, but not. Like all bent and deformed, and... and... strange looking."

Evelyn frowned over at me. I thought of the figure I'd seen near the clearing as we ran away. I gripped the shotgun tighter and checked the safety. It was on, at the moment. I could switch it off easily. Quickly, if I needed to. "Okay, Katie. I can understand why that was scary. Seeing something strange looking like that." She looked over at Ryan. "You didn't see it Ryan?" She asked tentatively.

"No" Ryan shook his head. "I saw nothing. Nothing at all." He ran a hand through his hair, sweeping it back off his forehead. "And I don't believe Katie did, either. It was probably a... a tree or something, in the shape of a person." He sneered at her, "I'm telling you, there was nothing there."

"Oh yeah? A tree?" Katie snorted. "Explain how it moved then."

"The wind, Katie," Ryan spat at her. "Dad is going to be so pissed." He shook his head and walked a few feet away, turning his back on us.

"That's not what I meant," Katie insisted, taking a step closer towards him, both fists clenched at her sides. "I meant, how did it follow us then?" She turned to look at Evelyn, then at me. "I saw it again. After I'd started running away. It was there." She pointed off to her left, back the way they had come from. "It was off to the side of us, it had moved, it ran after us." Ryan shook his head again, chucking. "I know what I saw, Ryan."

"You're delusional, Katie." Ryan turned back to face us. "You got spooked being in the woods, in the dark. Your imagination ran away with you, made you see things that weren't there. It's easy to do that out here, see shapes in the trees that aren't actually anything but shadows and branches." He shook his head at her again. "You shouldn't have come with us. You should've stayed home with Mom."

Katie ran a hand over her face and let out a shriek of frustration. "You are such an asshole sometimes."

"Katie," Evelyn murmured, admonishing her. She put a hand around Katie's shoulders. "Look, there's no point arguing like this." Evelyn shook her head at me. "I think the best thing to do right now is to go find the deer blind. Hook back up with our dads and see what they want to do." She looked up at the sliver of sky visible between the trees above us. "It's not that light out yet, maybe we can move to another location and have a shot still."

Katie and Ryan remained quiet. "What do you think, Teddy?" I was still staring up at the sky above, trying to judge how long we had left until daylight. Maybe 15 minutes tops, I thought, not long enough to make it back to the cars and move to another location entirely. I looked back at Evelyn and found they were all waiting for me to respond. I glanced around us, eyes on the woods surrounding our little group. I didn't spy any movement, or any sign of bent, twisted figures amongst the trees. But Ryan was right, it was easy enough to do, to imagine seeing something that wasn't there in the shadows between the trees.

I nodded to Evelyn. "I think that's for the best. I doubt we have enough time left until daylight to move to another location completely, but let's head back to the deer blind and see what they want to do."

Evelyn nodded, and Katie sighed, letting her begin to lead her forward. I knew the general direction of the deer blind from here and definitely from the location where Evelyn and I had been sitting by the fallen tree. I set off in that direction, and the others followed, Ryan bringing up the rear in silence.

6

K atie unleashed a barrage of hysteria when we arrived at the deer blind that left both my dad and Dr. M momentarily speechless. She demanded to know where her father was as they gaped at her, open mouthed.

Dad spoke up first, pointing off to the left. "He's over that way, about a quarter of a mile or so. He's set up in the smaller blind."

"Did you hear her screaming from here?" Ryan asked, eying Katie's back, his mouth a grim line. "I'm sure she's scared away the deer for a few miles around."

Dad and Dr. M looked at each other for a moment then turned back to us. "We thought we heard something a few minutes ago, yeah, but didn't know what it was." Dr. M shrugged. "It could've scared the deer away, they probably have better hearing than we do." He looked at me for a second. Eyes darting away again just as swiftly. He cleared his throat. "I mean, I think it might be best to move, but given the timing, do we just stay here for a bit at this point? What do you think, Jim?"

Dad was watching Katie still. She screwed up her hands into fists, bringing them up to her chest then slamming them down again, "Ugh! Why is everyone so concerned about the freaking deer?" She pointed back in the general direction we had come from. "There's a freaking... monster, back there, following us! Are you all insane?" She looked around at us, one at a time. And we all stared back at her. "We need to leave, now."

"Katie," Dr. M began, sighing, his voice trailing off. "We can't just leave; we came all this way..."

Katie shook her head. "You just don't believe me, that's all." Her shoulders slumped forward. "And it's freezing cold on top of it."

"Here," Dr. M said, holding the flap for the deer blind open for her, "why don't you come in here and try to warm up a little?" Katie sighed and Evelyn grabbed her arm, leading her into the deer blind. Evelyn exchanged a look with her dad and went into the blind after her.

Dad and Dr. M moved over towards Ryan and I once the girls were inside. "Did you guys see anything?"

Ryan shook his head immediately. "Nope. I was right there with her the whole time. Nothing." He shrugged. "I think it was just her imagination. Tree branches and a trick of the lighting." I watched Ryan, staying quiet. My mind went back over the rush to run after Evelyn. What had I seen, exactly? Was I sure it had been a figure standing there? Or is it possible my brain had done the same thing? Taken twisted tree branches and turned them into phantom limbs?

"Teddy?" I turned to realize Dad was watching me. A careful expression on his face. "Did you see something?" I just stared back at him mutely.

"He wasn't even there," Ryan said, exasperation edging into his voice.

"Well," Dr. M said, sighing, turning to Dad. "Are we going to stick it out here? Or do you want to move on?"

Dad looked over in the direction Dr. Carter was posted up in. He didn't answer for a moment. "Haven't heard from Dave yet," he said slowly. "Let's just stay here for now. We can always move on in a bit."

We spent the next hour or so waiting. Katie continued on about not being taken seriously, but managed to keep her voice down, with several reminders from Evelyn, that is. She fell silent eventually. I had ducked into the blind to sit with her for a bit when Ev needed a break. Katie seemed to have run out of things to complain about. She stared glumly down at her feet, eyes glazed over, lost in her own thoughts.

The forest around us remained quiet and still. As we stood beneath the boughs of a copse of massive pines, it began to dawn on me how little wildlife we had encountered. The silence of the woods became almost ominous after a while. Where I would normally expect to hear the faint high-pitched twittering of invisible birds flitting above our heads, high up in the trees, there was only the wind, blowing hollowly through the branches. The limbs surrounding us swayed gently back and forth, cavorting when the breeze picked up momentarily without warning. The chitter of squirrels, found in abundance back home, was also noticeably absent too. The forest maintained a beautiful but cold facade as though it were separate from us somehow. It felt like we were in it, but not part of it. We were trespassers here, and the forest paused. Watched us. Waited for us to leave.

Had we scared away all the wildlife between Katie's screaming and our frantic run through the underbrush? But that had been a while ago now. It didn't seem possible that could be the reason for the foreboding stillness engulfing us now.

I thought about what Mr. Johnson had said, about the disappearances in this part of the woods, and I shivered slightly. It was easy enough to imagine. Being alone, out in this forest, turned around, with no landmarks to guide your way. No wonder people went missing.

The forest would be treacherous at night. We had come across several drop-offs leading to jagged rocks and little gurgling streams. We weren't even in the mountains yet and still the terrain was anything but flat. It would be slow going and rough to traverse, especially at night without any source of light.

There was nothing supernatural about it, just as he had said. The wilderness didn't need any help to claim wayward travelers; there were plenty of natural dangers to snare anyone who entered here unprepared. I patted my chest, feeling for the compass and map, verifying they were still tucked in the inside pocket of my coat. Going off-trail like we were always held an inherent risk. Even when relatively close to civilization, it was easier than you'd think to get turned around and end up walking in circles.

Dad had made sure I knew how to use a compass, but more importantly, made sure I knew how to determine the cardinal directions from the sun. It always paid to have a back-up plan, as he was fond of saying. A compass can get lost, can break; never assume your gear will be there when you need it most. Adapt. Have an alternate route. Have an escape plan. Always assume the worst. Always assume things can and will go wrong, and you'll never be caught unprepared.

I heard footsteps suddenly, out of the quiet of the woods, pine needles and leaves crunching underfoot. I lifted the flap of the deer blind and poked my head out right at the same moment Dad reached out to grab the flap. "Hey kids, we're thinking we've spent enough time hanging around here. Let's pack up and head over to find your dad, Katie."

Katie nodded and pushed past me through the opening. "Fine by me. Trust me, I'm more than ready to get out of here. There's something wrong with these woods."

Dad had no response to that. He and Dr. M folded up the deer blind, and we watched in silence, Ryan stepping up eventually to help them, falling in line as we marched off to find Dr. Carter.

I followed behind Katie, at the tail end of the group. I turned repeatedly, keeping an eye on the still forest behind us, one hand grasped onto my shotgun slung over my right shoulder, the cold metal comforting in my hand. The thought echoed numbly from a remote corner of my mind, repeating over and over until it became the drum beat I marched to: *'There's something wrong with these woods. Something wrong with these woods. Something wrong with these woods.'*

7

— • —

D r. Carter had set up a smaller deer blind for himself, just as Dad had said. It was flimsy, blowing in the wind, slung between two trees. And it was empty.

He was nowhere in sight. We combed the area near the deer blind in silence. Katie and Evelyn stood arm in arm. Katie sighing, an impatient look on her face. It was just another setback in her return to the comfort of the house, a barrier keeping her out in the cold. Evelyn stood there next to her, her plump lips twisted in a frown, the tip of her nose bright red.

A confused look on Dad's face. I watched him as he walked slowly, carefully, searching the ground around the blind, looking for tracks to follow. I joined him, fanning out a distance away from the blind.

I headed over towards the nearest clearing. It was hardly a clearing, really, more of just a little break in the trees, besides a smattering of low bushes and tangled brambles under a copse of pine, the sort of place a deer might choose to bed down in.

About ten feet away, I found it. A splatter of blood on the ground, spread over long rust colored pine needles, the edges of fallen leaves painted red.

"Dad," I called out, my voice sounding too loud, too harsh, in the quiet of the woods. He scanned for me, and when he'd spotted me, I pointed down at the blood near my feet. He wasted no time, moving over to me in a light jog, shotgun bouncing on his back.

"What'd you find Teddy?" he asked, his words exiting in puffs of white.

I pointed again, nodding down at the ground. "Blood," I said. But he had already found it, crouching down for a closer look.

"Nice," he murmured after a moment. He straightened up and called over to the others. "He must have got a deer!" Dad surveyed the ground around the blood spatters, and we began to walk out in circles. We found more blood a few feet away. It looked like there was a scuffle here.

"Maybe the deer went down here momentarily?" I asked, frowning up at Dad, crouching down and touching the damp earth with two fingers. Leaves and pine needles had been disturbed, rich, dark earth turned up. He stared down at the ground, then back at me, nodding slowly. "I don't see any deer tracks..." I murmured, wiping the dirt off on my pant leg as I stood.

Dad was already moving past me, following the blood trail off to the right. "You got that compass, Teddy?" he asked, stretching his arm back to me, without looking. I reached in the pocket of my coat, and pulled out the compass, slapping it into his outstretched palm.

Evelyn moved over to my side, eyes combing the ground. She frowned at me, scratching her cheek with one hand, then reaching up to tug her hat down further over her ears. She'd been forced to don one of the bright orange beanies Dad had brought. Evelyn wasn't what I considered vain, as far as girls went, but I had overheard her complaining to Katie before we left that it clashed horribly with her red hair. I disagreed. I grinned at the hat, not realizing I was showing my thoughts on my face. She noticed and smacked me on the arm.

"Shut up," she said, grinning a little, although I hadn't said anything.

"I didn't say a word," I said, shrugging. But the corners of my lips tugged up in a grin, as she hit me again.

"You thought it," she said bluntly. "I could hear you thinking it." She rolled her eyes at me, then gestured to my dad, or to the blood droplets he was following. "Is this going to be enough to help us find him?"

I looked back down at the blood on the ground; the initial splattering of blood I had found looked like a significant amount. I gestured back towards it, "That's a decent amount of blood. My guess would be the deer wouldn't make it too much farther after losing that much blood." I shrugged, "It's hard to say for sure though. Depending on where it was shot, sometimes they can travel a ways, farther than you would think."

Evelyn eyed the blood on the ground and swallowed, nodding at my words. "Well, I guess I'm about to find out what it's like."

"What what's like?" I asked, frowning at her in confusion.

"Seeing a dead deer, I mean." She dropped her voice lower, glancing over at Ryan as she answered. He seemed to be oblivious, though. He stood there, gazing absentmindedly, surveying the woods around us, a content expression on his face. I stared at him, my brows creasing. A thought nagged at me, in the back of my mind, but I couldn't quite grasp it. Was it something I'd forgotten? Something I'd been about to say?

I turned back to Evelyn, as she tugged on the sleeve of my jacket. "Come on, we're leaving." She inclined her head to the side, and I followed her gesture to see the backs of our dads retreating off into the woods. Dad's arm outstretched as he held up the compass for a moment, then returned to watching the ground. Katie followed behind them, practically stomping her feet in exaggerated steps, head tilted back, and shoulders raised to her ears, eyes on the sky.

I followed after Evelyn, glancing up myself, to see clouds rolling overhead. Big fat, puffy clouds, heavy with moisture. I groaned a little. That was all we needed, for it to start raining. Katie would pitch a fit.

I glanced back to see Ryan had fallen into step behind us, one hand on his rifle, slung over his left shoulder. He caught me watching him and gave me a wicked looking grin, then winked, his left eye shuttering closed for a second in an almost corny, exaggerated gesture. I stared back at him, but he had already looked away, eyes down on his own feet, as he stepped carefully over tree roots.

The woods grew thicker here, and I found myself focusing on my own footsteps as we made our way through the underbrush. That nagging feeling returned as we walked, hovering in my periphery, like the flash of an image, just out of focus, that disappeared, retreating further as I tried to look at it directly.

I watched my boots moving, one foot after the other, stepping over gnarled roots and fallen branches. I listened to our feet rustling through the blanket of leaves, as we followed Dad, and the thinning trail of bright red droplets that led us on to Dr. Carter.

I eyed the bright red spatters suspiciously as we went. When Dad stopped at a particularly big splatter on some leaves at waist height, I stopped beside him, watching as he dipped a finger into the blood, and lifted it gingerly to his nose. He sniffed at it, and frowned down at the blood splatter, before reaching down to wipe his fingers on a clump of leaves.

"What is it?" I asked him, frowning, my heart starting to thump a little harder in my chest.

"I..." he trailed off for a second. "It's nothing. Nothing, Teddy." He reached in the pocket of his jeans and pulled out the battered compass, handing it to me. "Here, hold onto this for me." He looked back the way we had come, and then up ahead, at the others. They had moved past us, following Dr. M as he attempted to search for more blood amongst the fallen leaves. "We're headed northwest at the moment." Dad glanced at me, one eyebrow raised. "Do you think you could find the way back to our cars from here?"

I looked at him for a moment. Then sighed, tucking the compass back into the pocket in my coat.

"With the map, and the cars marked on there, and the compass... yeah, I think I could." I glanced up at the sky. Tracking the direction of the sun was a bit more difficult now, with the heavy clouds rolling overhead. I looked back at Dad, not sure what else he was looking for, or expecting, from my answer, but he seemed satisfied and just nodded absentmindedly.

"Let's keep going a bit farther, see if we come across him soon." I nodded in agreement, and we continued on. We walked for another five minutes or so, the droplets of blood becoming fewer and farther between, until they trickled out, and disappeared altogether.

Dad and Dr. M stood shoulder to shoulder, muttering back and forth, each gesturing in different directions. I could tell they disagreed, arguing over our next move. Now that the blood trail had run out, we'd be wandering blindly, so to speak. There were no obvious deer tracks to follow; hadn't been all along. Although the ground was fairly dry, it still seemed a little odd that we hadn't come across a track yet.

Evelyn sidled up to me, leaving Ryan to listen to Katie moaning about how much her feet hurt. I couldn't help but smile at her, a goofy grin on my face, as she approached me. "What?" An answering smile spread slowly across her face as she moved closer.

"Nothing." I shook my head, willing my features into a more serious mask, an absence of emotion. There was nothing to smile about at the moment.

Evelyn nodded in our dad's direction, to where they stood arguing, the volume of their voices starting to rise. I still couldn't make out any of their words, but I could hear the tone, and it didn't sound good. "They're arguing about what we should do next," she said quietly to me, biting her bottom lip. "Your Dad seems to think we should turn around, head back to the cars." She glanced up at the sky as she spoke. "It is starting to look a little dark, isn't it?" Wrinkles creased between her brows. "I don't love the look of those clouds."

I followed her gaze, the dark heavy underbelly of a low cloud roiling above our heads. "No," I agreed, "I don't either."

"What do you think we should do?" she murmured, looking worried now. "We can't just leave Dr. C out here all alone." She looked back in Katie and Ryan's direction. "Somehow, I doubt he could find his way on his own." She frowned. "Not to mention, we can't all fit in one car. What are we going to do, leave him stranded here all alone with no way to get home?"

I just shook my head, frowning over at my dad. Was he really saying we should just leave? That seemed a little premature. I glanced down at my wrist, shrugging the sleeve of my shirt up, and looking briefly at my watch, before catching the stock of the shotgun again against my elbow as it began to slide forward. "It doesn't make any sense," I agreed. "It's only been a few hours. We have hours of daylight left, even if it does get dark earlier out here." I shook my head, and Evelyn's frown deepened at my words.

"Teddy," I turned to see Dad and Dr M were making their way over to us, "Let's see that map for a minute."

I pulled out the map from my pocket and handed it over to them. They studied it for a moment, holding it upright in the air as best they could, Evelyn and Dr. M reaching out and grabbing hold of the edges to help keep it steady in the wind. "So, we're somewhere here." Dad pulled a glove off, using his finger to indicate our relative position on the map. "We should come across this little stream here soon." He indicated up ahead, "If we stick to continuing on, following the direction the blood trail was leading us in, that takes us further northwest, closer to Glastenbury Mountain." He glanced up at the sky. "It looks like it might rain, or snow..." he trailed off, eyeing all of us in turn. "Some of us are more prepared for inclement weather than others." He cleared his throat. "But we may have some extra gear back in the SUV."

Dr. M thought for a moment, nodding. He eyed Evelyn. "I say we continue on, at least until we come to the stream. See if he's in the general area, then we can always head back to the cars, grab whatever we need." Dad nodded in agreement, and the map was re-folded, and handed back to me. I tucked it away again, and we continued in relative silence with Katie interjecting commentary every now and then. Evelyn stayed nearby, walking in tandem beside me as we followed Dad's lead, in search of the little mountain stream up ahead.

We never made it there. Dr. Carter stepped out, seemingly from nowhere, off to my left. I jumped about a half mile as I caught the sudden movement and flash of color out of the corner of my eye.

"There you are!" he called to us, his cheerful tone of voice ringing hollowly out of place. The group froze and turned as one. He stood there, a lopsided grin on his face. His clothing looked oddly rumpled, as though he had been running, or fallen down and gotten all out of sorts. His long brown hair was mussed, glasses slightly askew. He was breathing heavily, and he was covered in blood.

A swath of red painted his chest and stomach, blood smeared all down the arms of his jacket. He was empty handed, his gun nowhere in sight.

"Dave?" Dad was the first to speak, his voice held a note of uncertainty. "Is everything okay?"

"Yeah." Dr. Carter held his hands out, shrugging, "Of course! I got a deer!" He grinned again, studying us now, eyes flickering over each of us in turn. "Everything okay with you all?" he asked, frowning slightly.

"Yes," Dr. Montgomery said slowly, "We're fine. We just… we've been looking everywhere for you." His eyes trailed up and down Dr. C, taking in the blood stains, lingering on his empty hands. "Where's your gun?" he asked, brows creasing.

Dr. Carter frowned again, then pointed off in the distance. "I left it sitting over there, set it down against a tree. Why?" He shrugged again, then started to turn, not waiting for a response. "Come on." He gestured us on with a waving motion. I can't possibly carry this thing myself." He chuckled, "Trust me, I tried." He pivoted back towards us, indicating the blood all over his chest. "It's going to take the three of us at least. We might need help from Ryan and Teddy too."

He began to walk off into the trees. He stopped after a few feet, glancing back at us to see no one had moved. "You coming or what?" He chuckled again, waving us on, and shook his head as the group started to follow.

Dr. M and Ryan started after him, followed close behind by Katie. "God, Dad, way to make us wander all over the woods. A note would have been nice." She rolled her eyes as she passed me.

Dad seemed to hesitate another moment, then sighed, and shrugged his shoulders as he fell in line after them. Evelyn rolled her eyes at me and grinned. "Yay, more walking." She brushed past my shoulder, calling "You coming Teddy?"

I sighed and hiked up the shotgun strap over my shoulder, and followed after her, a sense of unease curling in the pit of my stomach. I took a deep breath. Great. The last thing I needed was to have an anxiety attack out here. There would be nowhere to hide. I eyed the dark clouds overhead wearily, and followed the group, deeper into the wilderness.

8

— • —

I'll be the first to admit that I suffer from an odd sort of time-blindness. Hours can feel like minutes for me, and vice versa. I often lose track of time, and I'm always running late because of it, but I felt certain it had been an hour at least at this point.

We traipsed through the dense wood, following Dr. Carter's back as he led us on, the terrain getting rougher, and rockier as we went. I wasn't the only one getting impatient, either. Dad had stopped him several times to ask if he was sure we were going the right way. It seemed hard to believe that the deer had traveled this far after being shot. He'd recounted the story for us, twice, and while I couldn't put my finger on anything out of the ordinary, I somehow just... didn't believe him.

It took me a while to sort that out, to recognize what I was feeling. I had taken it for that all too familiar edge of panic drawing closer. The dread of yet another wave of irrational fear looming in my near future.

With nothing else to do but think as we walked through the oddly quiet woods, it eventually dawned on me that the feeling was externally driven, not coming from that inexplicable well buried inside of me, but from something else. Something that had nothing to do with me, and everything to do with Dr. Carter.

We had come to and crossed that stream Dad was aiming for, and I could tell from the direction of the sun that Dr. C was leading us further northwest, closer to Glastenbury Mountain. I pulled the compass out of my pocket at one point, discreetly, and verified I was right.

He kept insisting that it was just a little bit further, that we were almost there, but I couldn't help but feel a creeping sense of unease. It was almost as though he was leading us on purposefully, taking us further into the woods.

The terrain here was rough, as we were starting to head up-hill, which slowed our pace significantly. That nagged at me too. Would an injured deer really head uphill like this? It would make more sense to take the path of least resistance.

Dad seemed to be echoing my thoughts, perpetuating my anxiety as he sighed deeply and came to a stop once again. "Dave," he called out, his voice held an edge of exasperation now. "Come on man, admit you don't know where the deer is. We've been walking for over an hour now... maybe it's time we give up and move on."

I frowned at his words and saw Evelyn eyeing my expression wearily. The timeframe didn't make any sense.

Maybe that was what was bothering me. Say he had shot the deer almost immediately after posting up this morning, in the time it took for Katie to see... whatever it was she saw, start screaming, then for the four of us to meet up and go join our dads, sit with them for an hour or so... was it physically possible? Could he have walked this far following the deer and made it all the way back to where he found us in that time? It didn't seem likely, at least.

It hit me then like a punch to the gut, the other thing that had been bothering me, nagging at the back of my mind. My heart started to beat louder, *thump-thumping* in my ears. I took a deep steadying breath, willing my pulse to slow, willing myself to calm down.

Dr. Carter turned and sighed, laughing a little. He surveyed the group, then shrugged. "I swear." He chuckled again. "It's got to be right around here somewhere. Maybe we split up? Fan out in circles in this area? That might help us come across it faster." He reached up with his left hand, using his thumb and pointer finger to slide his glasses up the bridge of his nose.

I felt a jolt of fear and panic course through my chest, my gut. Before I knew what I was doing, I slid my hand from where it had gripped the shotgun, now damp with sweat, and raised it in one smooth motion, leveling it at his chest, my finger sliding into place, hovering over the trigger.

The reaction from the group was immediate, but I barely registered them consciously. I was remotely aware of Dad stepping forward, a hand outstretched. Evelyn bringing her hands up to cover her mouth. Katie calling out something to me.

I was locked onto him, onto Dr. Carter. He didn't even flinch. Not a flicker of surprise across his features. He met my eyes, his face blank, completely void of expression, his eyes cold and fathomless.

I felt a fissure of fear slicing open a gaping hole in my chest, but my arms, my hands, were steady.

"The gunshot," I said, my voice sounding steadier, calmer, than I had expected.

The group fell utterly and completely silent. No one moved, nothing stirred in the woods surrounding us. Only the gentle swaying of tree branches, limbs waving in time with the wind. Dr. Carter's expressionless eyes stayed locked on mine.

"Did anyone hear the gunshot?" I said, keeping my voice as steady as possible.

"Teddy," Dad said, both arms raised, hands held out to me, palms out. "Put the gun down, Teddy. What are you talking about son?"

I licked my lips, dry in the cold mountain air. I didn't move otherwise. "There was no gunshot this morning. You were, what, three quarters of a mile away from us at the most? There was no gunshot. Not that I heard, at least." I raised my voice louder, speaking to the group, "Did anyone hear a gunshot?"

"Teddy." Dr. Carter held his hands up and took a step towards me. I flicked off the safety, never taking my eyes off of him.

"Teddy, what the hell are you doing?" Ryan's voice jumped out at me from the chorus of voices all clamoring at once. Dr. C stared back at me, neither of us moving.

"No." I heard Evelyn's voice as an expectant silence fell again. "He's right. There was no gunshot this morning. I didn't hear anything. Did any of you?"

Silence again. No one spoke for seconds that stretched on in aching slowness. Then Dad's voice, closer now, off to my right. "I didn't hear it either," he admitted, his voice flat, but with an edge of uncertainty.

"We were a quarter mile away; we should have heard it," Dr. M added.

"So, you're going to shoot my dad, because you didn't hear his gun go off this morning?" Katie said, her voice dripping with fear and confusion.

"That's not your Dad," I said quietly, the words coming out of my mouth instinctually without a second thought. But I knew they were true, as soon as I'd spoken them. And I felt a shiver go down my spine.

"What?" Katie sputtered. "What do you mean that's not my Dad?"

Dr. C's eyes were like two black holes in his head. Ryan moved closer to me, off to my left. I didn't move a muscle. "What the fuck is that supposed to mean Ted?" I could tell when the volume of his voice dropped off that he had turned away from me. "I told you. Last night. I fucking told you." I knew he was talking to Evelyn. My gut twisted, but I didn't move.

"Dave." Dr. Montgomery spoke next, his voice dangerously quiet and calm, with an edge of a threat to it. "Did you shoot a deer this morning?"

I could sense everyone still behind me, waiting. Dr. Carter finally took his eyes off of me, scanning the others, until, I'm assuming, landing on Dr. Montgomery. I didn't turn to look.

He smiled. A slow, odd smile, like the muscles around his mouth were out of practice, unused to stretching. "Of course I did. Where do you think all this blood came from?" He held his arms out, and his gaze flickered to the side, for the briefest of seconds, off into the woods to my right.

A howl ripped through us, from shockingly close by. So close it made my blood recoil, stoking some ancient, instinctual fear that was on a level I hadn't previously known existed. Pandemonium. Panic. I had turned to the right, taking my eyes off of him involuntarily when that howl rocked through the forest, and I recognized the mistake I had made a split second too late. I turned back, bringing the muzzle of the shotgun back to position, to where Dr. Carter had been standing just a second before.

He was already gone, moving too fast. Unnaturally fast, as he exploded away, bounding on limbs that bent at an odd angle, springing onto a rocky ledge off to the left, that I knew in my gut was too high, far too high for a human to jump to. He scrambled over the rocks above, disappearing over the hill, and was gone.

9

— • —

The howl was followed by a second, and then a third. All off to our right, echoing through the trees. The others had pulled their guns by now.

But there was nothing visible. Nothing to aim at. I kept the muzzle of my gun trained to the left, over and to the side of the rocky hill Dr. Carter had disappeared behind.

We fell back, moving into a huddled group, falling away from the wall of trees hiding the source of the reverberating howling that continued, growing steadily closer.

"Teddy, the compass." Dad held a hand out to me, and I pulled it out quickly. He grabbed it and oriented to our position. "This way!" he called out to us, and we turned, and started running.

We ran fast at first, but the group could only sustain that pace for so long. Thankfully, the howls retreated more comfortably into the distance, reassuring us that whatever it was making the ethereal spine-tingling sounds wasn't keeping pace with us.

We slowed eventually to a light jog, and then to a walk, as Katie called out, holding onto her side, "I can't..." she breathed, leaning forward. "I need to stop for a second." We slowed further and came to a halt. Everyone was breathing heavily. Dr. Montgomery gasping for breath. I turned to face the direction we'd fled from, holding my shotgun aloft, off to the side, but at the ready.

But the howling seemed to have stopped. There was nothing but the relative silence of the wind through the trees, and our rapid breathing, producing white puffs in the air. I was covered in a light sheen of sweat, rapidly cooling, causing the air to feel even colder than it had before.

Evelyn held her hands together in front of her, shivering slightly, jaw clenched tight, and eyes wide. She watched me, a cautious expression on her face. She met my eyes for a moment before turning away. I felt my chest cave in a little. I turned to find Ryan glaring at me, eyes cold beneath dark brows.

"Okay," Dad said breathlessly, still panting slightly. He held the compass aloft again. "We're heading in the right direction, back to the cars. We don't have to run, but let's keep going, at a steady pace."

"And what's next? We drive away, and just leave Dad out here all alone?" Katie panted, eyes narrowed.

"We can't all fit in one car," Dr. M mumbled to Dad.

I opened my mouth to protest, but I could feel it. Evelyn's doubt. Ryan's disgust. I was sure, though. I was sure I was right. Even if it sounded crazy. Even if it made no sense. "That wasn't him," I insisted, my voice sounding small.

"Then who the hell was it, Teddy?" Ryan spun on me. "Huh? Who was it then?" He laughed. "Just some other dude who looks and sounds like him, who knows all of our names? What the hell are you even talking about?"

"Okay, okay." Dad held a hand up, stepping between us. "Let's just calm down, okay."

"Then why'd he run, Ryan?" I stepped forward, my voice rising. "Why did he just run away? He took off the second I was distracted. Did you see him?" I could tell by his face that he hadn't. "Did any of you see him? How fast he moved?" I was yelling now. I couldn't help it. "I'm telling you, that wasn't him! I have no clue who or what that was, but that was not Dr. Carter."

Evelyn still eyed me wearily, but her expression was more thoughtful now, as though she was considering my words, as though she could feel a ring of truth to them.

Ryan shook his head, chuckling. "You're crazy man."

"Okay, Ry, that's enough." Dr. M stepped forward. "I'm not sure what's happening here, but we're all a little freaked out, okay. I think we need to focus on getting back to the cars, away from whatever the heck is howling over there."

We came to an uneasy truce and continued our trek back to the cars.

I could feel Ryan's eyes on me though, could feel him watching me, and I watched him back.

I felt the group breathe a collective sigh of relief as we finally sighted the cars in the distance, the sheen of metal between the trees a welcome sight.

Dad pulled his car keys out of the pocket of his jeans and hit the unlock button as we approached. Everyone murmured at once as doors were pulled open. Katie climbed into the backseat of Dr. M's truck, slumping down with a grateful sigh.

I was slightly surprised to see there were no other vehicles parked near ours. I added to the list of things that had been making me uneasy as I frowned at the small clearing.

It was opening day. Why wasn't it busier? Why wasn't the forest flooded with hunters? My mind flipped back through the events of the weekend. I recalled Dr. M talking with Dad and Dr. Carter yesterday, as he explained where we would drive in, where we would park. He had wanted to head to the Glastenbury Wilderness rather than the tract of forest that lay just to the west of Mount Snow. It was more easily accessible, but more heavily trafficked. He had decided on this location purposefully, hoping the larger, untouched vastness of the area would lead to a more successful hunt. Heading further off the beaten path, to an area that was less accessible would hopefully mean less people hunting, but we'd run into no one out in the woods; hadn't come across a single flash of orange.

Dad approached me and wordlessly handed me a water bottle. I took it and sipped gratefully. He watched me for a moment. I could tell he was getting ready to say something.

"Holy shit!" I heard Dr. M exclaim. He was crouched down at the back of his truck, examining one of the back tires. "I can't fucking believe this." He looked over at us. "Someone slashed the tires. Why would they do that?" He stood and ran a hand through his hair, staring at his truck.

Dad moved over to our SUV, crouching down, running a hand along the left rear tire. "You've gotta be kidding me," he murmured.

"Yours too?" Dr. M spun to him. "Fuck!" He kicked the now useless tire of his truck.

"What?" Katie yelped, her voice muffled. She sat up, scrambling out of the back seat, coming around to the rear of the truck, and then heading to the front.

But Ryan was already there, having circled around from the other side. "The front tires are slashed too," he called out.

Dad moved quickly to the driver's side door, pulling it open, he climbed halfway into the SUV, and stuck the key in the ignition, cranking it to the right. I watched in silent horror as nothing happened. He cranked it back, turning the key again, several times, but nothing. No rumbling, no engine roaring to life. He let out an exasperated sound, slamming his hands on the steering wheel.

Dr. Montgomery watched as well, moving quickly over to climb into the truck. He slammed the door shut behind him. I watched him through the glass as he copied Dad's motions, watched as he let out what was probably a string of expletives. I saw him pull his cell phone out and watched as he sat there, staring at it, poking buttons, and holding it up in the air. Dad had said he had no signal on his phone back at the house. I couldn't imagine there would be out here.

Dr. M threw the phone down on the passenger seat after a few seconds. He sat there for a moment afterwards, thinking, before climbing out, slowly shutting the door again behind him, and moving over to where Dad now stood, a few feet in front of the SUV, watching him.

Dad motioned to him and the two of them walked off a ways, muttering and gesturing to each other animatedly.

This went on for several minutes. They were out of earshot, for me, at least, and I ignored them after a bit. I walked a ways away myself, heading in the other direction, to the rear of our cars, and off towards the treeline. I stood there, eyes on the sky, still dark with heavy clouds rolling endlessly by. I really hoped it wasn't going to rain. The weather forecast hadn't called for anything, I knew because we triple checked. Dad had still made me bring an extra case for my hearing aids. He'd told me to carry it with me, just in case; water and hearing aids don't mix well. But I'd left it in my backpack, of course. Best I could do was take them off and leave them in the car or shove them in a pocket.

I heard a crunch of footsteps just behind me and turned swiftly to find Evelyn standing there. She paused, eyes flickering to the shotgun I still held off to one side. I sighed and licked my lips, trying to come up with something to say to her, something to explain what surely seemed like odd behavior, something to make her see what I saw, make her understand.

But I had nothing, nothing at all, at the moment. I slung the shotgun strap over my shoulder, letting it fall against my back. "The safety is back on, if that makes you feel any better." I heard myself muttering to her, and I colored instantly, feeling my cheeks, which must be already red with cold, heat slightly.

Evelyn's face crumpled in a bit, and she shook her head, eyes darting away from me. "Teddy..." she trailed off. "About last night, I was trying to tell you... I was trying to tell you that I didn't agree with him. With Ryan. I was trying to tell you that I don't think you're like that." She met my eyes again. "That I trust you." I swallowed, staring into her green eyes. Her cheeks were flushed from the cold.

I watched her as she spoke, her voice heavy with emotion, as tiny, perfect snowflakes started to fall, dusting her frizzy red curls, peeking out under her orange hat, falling on her upturned nose, her cheeks, dusting her eyelashes, dispersing when she blinked. Her green eyes were wide and solemn as she watched me back, eyes darting back and forth over mine, as though she was reading something there, written on my features. Something I couldn't say.

"Evelyn, I..." I started, and she moved closer to me, then closer again, until she was only inches away.

"You what?" she asked huskily, and I felt her breath envelop me, clouding the air between us in white tendrils that disappeared like smoke.

"I..." I tried again, my breath a cloud, carried away in the wind, but the words wouldn't come to me. I studied her face, adorned with snowflakes, her parted lips, and the tips of her teeth peeking out between them. The perfect freckles on the bridge of her nose and speckled under her eyes.

"Teddy, I feel so bad you overheard us, and like I said, I just wanted you to know..."

I watched her as she spoke, losing track of her words. I couldn't even follow what she was saying. She was the most beautiful thing I'd ever seen. So beautiful it was painfully distracting. So beautiful, I could fall down at her feet and worship the ground she walked on. She paused suddenly, staring back at me, waiting for a response. I willed her silently to speak again. To say anything. I'd listen to her talk, forever, just to watch her lips moving. To hear her voice. I'd do anything for her. Anything.

"You..." I started again, reaching up a hand, I brushed the knuckles of two fingers along her cheek, dusting away the snowflakes crystalized there. She turned slightly, following the motion, turning towards my hand. I froze, and so did she, eyes like two pools of green, pulling me in.

Then I reached up and touched the curl along the side of her face, tucking it back, behind her ear. Her lips parted, and I leaned forward, imperceptibly, gravitating towards her, an invisible pull.

"Great!" Katie popped up out of nowhere, shattering the frozen moment we had been lost in. Her words pulled us back, out of the reverie, to our current, quickly spiraling situation.

Evelyn took a step back, away from me, as Katie pushed her way between us, a tear streaking down her cheek. She reached up and wiped it hastily away with a gloved hand.

"The freaking cars won't start, and they have no clue what to do." She pointed back towards Dad and Dr. M. "And now, it's starting to freaking snow!" Another tear coursed down her cheek. "We are going to freaking freeze out here!" Katie dissolved into a fit of tears, both hands over her face. Evelyn pulled her into her arms, tucking her head against her shoulder, she patted her on the back, and murmured to her.

I sighed, and turned away, eyeing Dad and Dr. M. They still stood on the other side of our cars, arguing louder now. I moved a little closer, away from the girls. Ryan was leaning against the bed of the truck. Both hands in his pockets, rifle slung at his side, staring glumly down at his feet.

I could make out some of their words now. I strained to listen. "I'm not standing around outside all night... sleep... freezing cold... nowhere." Dr. M seemed to be getting more and more agitated. Dad saw me watching them, and called out to me, waving a hand. I joined them as they reached the truck. "Teddy let's get that map out again. We have a decision to make."

10

— • —

We studied the map at length. Deliberating for some time over the best course of action. Based on the scale, we estimated a walk of at least ten miles, possibly closer to 12 or 13, back to civilization.

The closest heavily populated area to walk to would be Mount Snow. Granted, it was highly unlikely anyone would be around; there hadn't been significant snowfall yet this season. But we might come across an emergency phone that we could make a call from somewhere on the property. Either way, the rental house we were staying in wasn't too much farther from there, just a few streets over.

That distance was assuming a straight shot through the woods, not taking into consideration the elevation and what the terrain might be like. Following the road out would take us far out of the way, to the south and down around to the southeast, looping around the southern end of the Green Mountain National Forest. That route would more than double the distance we would need to walk.

Of course, sticking to the road greatly lessened our chances of getting lost, and it gave us a shot of running into someone driving out in this direction.

It was 1:30 now and the sun would start to set around 4:30. It would be fully dark by 5:00, at the latest. That left us with only three hours or so left of daylight; nowhere near long enough for us to make it out by either route before dark.

Dad and Dr. M had argued back and forth over whether it made more sense to stay with the cars and sleep inside overnight. They also debated setting up next to the cars in the clearing, which would allow us to start a fire, but Dr. M was worried we would be freezing in the cars, and there would be no way we could sleep out in the open next to the fire, not with just two sleeping bags and no tent.

It was snowing lightly but steadily now and the sky above us remained grey and overcast. Dad and Dr. M had us pull everything out of the vehicles, anything and everything, and we took inventory of our supplies.

Dad and I had two sleeping bags that folded up compact into drawstring bags. We had one large flashlight; the batteries worked, for now. We had a backpack, packed with some snacks, and a sandwich each. Which, thank God, Mrs. Michelle and Mrs. Sandy had thought to pack for us for lunch.

There was a plastic water bottle for each of us. There was a decent first aid kit and a little survival kit that Dad always kept in the SUV. It was stocked with a few matches, flint and steel, a whistle, a little pair of scissors, and fishing line and hook. We also had a raincoat, a sweatshirt, and a wooden baseball bat. In addition, we had the gun case which held the handgun, extra shotguns, and ammo.

We decided ultimately, given the cold and limited daylight, that it made the most sense to head back towards Glastenbury Mountain, to the abandoned village there. We could find shelter and hopefully find a building with a fireplace we could safely start a fire in to keep us warm overnight.

Dad and Dr. M argued again after we folded up the map. Dad was up for just staying in the cars for the night but given they wouldn't start and, given Dr. M's insistence, we ultimately decided against it. It wasn't worth the risk of being freezing cold all night.

Katie cried again, harder this time, at the thought of having to walk all the way back in the direction we had just come from. I cursed inwardly and at least felt that this was confirmation we were making the right decision to stay in the woods for the night.

If it had been just Dad and I, I think we could have gone for it; tried to walk out and make it to Mount Snow, used the flashlight once it got dark. But it was too far for the group. Everyone was already tired, fading fast, going on no food, little water, and having already walked for several hours.

We fell into line, marching to the sound of Katie's sniffles. Ryan was actually trying to be helpful for once. He'd tried comforting Katie and walked holding her hand for the first few minutes of the trek. He held the baseball bat loosely in his other hand.

Dad had chuckled slightly when he'd grabbed it to bring it with us, but Ryan had just shrugged and said, "I'm not the best shot, but I can swing a bat. If any of those wolves try to come at us, I probably have a better chance with this." Katie had sobbed even louder at that little comment.

Dad had chosen to grab the extra shotgun over the handgun. I was a little surprised, but I guessed the shotgun could probably do more damage. And I knew he was far more familiar with it. It meant we only needed to carry shells, as well. He tucked the handgun back into the gun case, relocking it.

We threw on any additional clothing we had available. Dad made Katie pull the spare raincoat on over her jacket. I had found a knit hat that I'd left in the car, tucked under my seat this morning. I hated wearing hats, but I pulled it out and put it on, pulling it down low over my ears. Thankfully the snow wasn't as bad as rain when it came to my hearing aids.

As prepared as we were ever going to be, we'd set off. That was about an hour or so ago now. We'd listened to Katie's sniffles and snuffles along the way, none of us speaking unless it was necessary. I was keeping my eyes peeled, studying the woods around us as we went, a thin layer of snow now coating the forest floor.

My mind kept returning to the standoff with Dr. Carter. To the coldness in his eyes. How he had run away, rather than face being questioned about the gunshot. How he'd used his left hand, his thumb and pointer finger, to push his glasses back up. Wrong hand, and wrong fingers. How many times had I seen him do that, just this weekend alone? That movement was a habit, set in stone. He'd never used his left hand. Not once. Sure, it wasn't much to go on, but I knew I had been right. I could tell from his reaction.

Where was he now? Was he out there in the woods, somewhere nearby? Was he watching us right now?

I scanned the forest around us once more, catching Evelyn's eye as I turned. I thought back to the moment we had earlier, how there had been so much I wanted to say to her, but I just couldn't, somehow. It hadn't really been the time though, or the place for it. Had I really been about to kiss her just before Katie interrupted us? It was like I'd been under a spell, and she had snapped me out of it. It had been a strange day, all around.

I eyed Ryan's back. I'd slowed my pace a bit, after a while, acting like I was getting tired. I gave everyone a chance to get ahead of me. Because that nagging feeling was still there, lingering in the background. I had thought confronting Dr. Carter would make it go away. And it had eased slightly, but it was back. Teasing me. Fading to a nerve-wracking background hum.

But of course, we were all a little on edge; our nerves beginning to fray. Evelyn had stepped on a branch at one point, and it snapped underfoot. Katie had yelped, jumping a few feet to the side. She'd perked up slightly after that, laughing a little at herself. It was how I imagined we all were feeling at the moment: on alert, waiting for the howling to start up again, waiting for Dr. Carter, or worse, to materialize out of the woods.

But we continued on at a steady pace, moving slowly closer to Glastenbury Mountain and the snow continued to fall around us. The extra blanket on the forest further muffled the travel of ambient sounds. The wind had died down slightly as well. I was grateful for that, as it left me feeling less cold than I had been earlier. But between that and the snow, the forest felt even more still, as though the woods itself was holding its breath, waiting for something to happen.

That feeling that we were strangers here in the woods, separate, a foreign 'other,' only deepened the longer we walked. While I wasn't sure what we would find waiting for us in the abandoned mountain town, I found myself looking forward to our arrival; I was ready to get out of these woods. Sick of the sight of the silent trees standing vigil surrounding us. To be inside, even in an old ramshackle, rundown house, felt like a welcome alternative.

We stopped to check the map multiple times and used the compass as we walked. From what I could tell, we were headed in the right direction, and I did trust Dad to get us there, eventually. The only question was whether we would find the town before nightfall.

I could sense the others getting anxious. The last time Dad stopped to check the map again, walking around with the compass, checking the position of the sun, I could read the anxiety on Evelyn's face. Even Dr. Montgomery looked worried, his expression strained. Katie was close to a breakdown. She kept repeating that she simply didn't know if she could walk any further.

Ryan seemed to be the only one who appeared relatively unaffected. He strolled in circles, swinging the bat idly. He even made a comment about carrying Katie, if she truly couldn't walk anymore. I gave Evelyn a sidelong look at that, but she didn't seem to think it was odd, or she just wasn't paying attention. She looked away from me hastily, a distracted sort of smile on her face. I had caught her staring at me several times. She said she trusted me, but there was a wariness in her eyes, a hint of something I couldn't place, that made me think otherwise.

When we finally found the town, it happened suddenly. I had expected to see buildings up ahead of us, in the distance, to know we were nearly there. Instead, we emerged over the crest of a tree covered hill to find a little valley. A nearly dry riverbed ran down the middle, and two large buildings sat on either side. A worn-down wooden bridge spanned the gap to either bank.

It could hardly be called a town, given it was really just a couple of buildings. I had expected it to feel ominous, unwelcoming. But the location felt cozy, if nothing else. Like a little secret, nestled into the valley, framed by two small peaks in the background.

Dad told us to hang out by the bridge, to wait until he and Dr. M took a look around and checked out the buildings. Katie sat down on a large rock with a sigh, stretching and massaging her legs.

"You made it Katie," Ryan said, reaching out and patting her on the back. "See, it wasn't so bad." He grinned down at her, but she didn't look up at him.

She sighed again, loudly. "Speak for yourself."

When Dad and Dr. M returned, they had apparently deliberated on their own, and decided we would spend the night in the old boarding house, which had been converted at some point to a hotel. It was the larger of the two buildings. I didn't know if Dad had to break in, or if he'd found the door unlocked, but the door handle turned, and the door opened easily when he led us inside.

We filed in past him as he held it open for us, Ryan and I bringing up the rear. "Come on in, boys," he murmured, his voice sounding tired and strained.

It was actually sort of cool, being inside the hotel. Or it would have been, under different circumstances. It had the look and feel of a museum. I guess because that's the only place I'd ever seen similar furniture. Dad made us promise to stay in the main lobby for now. He and Dr. M planned to explore upstairs to decide if it would be a good idea for us to sleep up there tonight. He eyed the stairs wearily, and I could understand why. They looked untrustworthy, with some holes punched through.

For now, we decided the best course of action would be to gather some firewood and get a fire going. Dr. M and Dad argued over whether the fire should be outside, or in the fireplace in the hotel. There was a large stone fireplace in the lobby and Dr. M was all for using it, but Dad was a little nervous about accidentally setting the building on fire. Dr. M must have won. Dad called out to me, "Teddy, will you go look for some firewood?" I nodded and turned to leave. "Bring your shotgun, and stick closer to the treeline, will you?"

"Yeah," I called back to him. I hadn't set my shotgun down yet, so I continued on my way out the door. We hadn't heard any howling on the way here, thankfully, and for all of my scanning, I hadn't seen anything out of the ordinary.

"I'll come with you," Evelyn called out. I turned, in what I hoped was a subtle way, to look at Dr. M. He met my eyes for a moment, then nodded. I flushed slightly as Evelyn jogged over, catching us looking at each other, but she said nothing. I guess it felt a little sexist, but given the circumstances, I wanted to make sure he was okay with it.

I stepped back out into the biting wind, suppressing a shudder. It wasn't exactly warm in the run-down hotel, but it was a few degrees warmer than being outside, and at least it provided shelter from the elements. Evelyn and I made our way over to the edge of the woods, neither of us speaking on the way there.

It wasn't too hard to find firewood; branches lay everywhere, and there were a few smaller fallen trees in the area. The hard part would be making sure the wood was dry enough to burn. "Let's shake all the snow off the branches before we bring them inside," I said, turning to Evelyn. "Hopefully the wood will be dry enough to burn."

Evelyn raised an eyebrow and nodded, dusting off the branch she was picking up. "I forgot about that," she murmured.

She moved a little closer to me, brows creased, and I stilled, watching her. "Teddy, I wanted to talk to you, about earlier." We'd been interrupted by Katie before anything happened, but... was she upset with me? For touching her cheek, her hair? She looked upset now. My gut twisted, and I let out a sigh.

"With Dr. Carter..." she started, then trailed off. "How can you be so sure it wasn't him?" I looked away from her, off into the distance. That wasn't what I'd been expecting her to say. I thought about it for a moment. "I believe you," she added, moving forward and grabbing my arm. "Teddy, I believe you." She forced me to look into her eyes, tugging on my arm until I turned to her. "I mean it. I believe *you* believe it, but I just want to know why."

I studied her eyes, thinking. "It's a lot of little things, more than one, big thing." I shrugged. "I don't know Evelyn, it's sort of hard to explain. I..." I wanted to look away again, started to, but she tugged on my arm again, gently, pulling me closer. "I just... notice things, sometimes. About people. Little things, I guess. Maybe..." I trailed off again, uncertain how to put it into words. I wanted to tell her the truth, to tell her enough, but not too much. I didn't want to sound stupid. Or crazy.

"Maybe sometimes, things that not everyone notices." I paused, licking my lips, shifting my eyes away from her steady gaze. "I noticed Dr. Carter has certain habits, there are certain things he does, that we all do. We all have habits like that. Little tells. The way we move, like muscle memory." I was rambling now, probably not making much sense. But she was nodding, expression thoughtful.

I sighed deeply. "Dr. Carter, he always pushes his glasses up, with his right hand, and his middle finger. It's sort of odd. Like a habit or a nervous tick he has. He does it the same way every time. Earlier, he used his left hand, his pointer finger and thumb... he never." I stopped, realizing I did sound crazy. "But it wasn't just that, it was the gunshot, too. Something kept bothering me, but I couldn't figure out what. Until it hit me suddenly, there wasn't a gunshot. So where did all that blood come from?"

Evelyn's brows creased further, and she broke eye contact for the first time, scanning the woods around us. "It was even the way he moved. The way he walked. It was similar, but not exactly...

right." I sighed again, running a hand through my hair. "I don't know, Ev. I know I sound crazy. But I..."

She shook her head, eyes finding mine again. "No, Teddy. It's not that, it's just..." She paused, her expression thoughtful for a second. "It's just that I had a bad feeling, too, like something wasn't right. But I never would have come to the same conclusion you did. I never would have decided, or thought, that it wasn't really him. I guess that part, I just... I'm having a hard time wrapping my mind around it. Not just that you thought it, but... but what does it mean? If that wasn't Dr. Carter, who was it?"

We heard a crunching, snapping sound, and both turned at the same moment, to see Ryan moving towards us. "Hey!" he called out, "I figured you could use some help."

I saw Evelyn's eyes narrow imperceptibly as she stared at him, and felt my gut tighten.

"Thanks, Ry," Evelyn called back as he moved closer. "Come on, let's get this over with." She shuddered slightly. "I'm so sick of being cold."

11

— • —

We sat huddled by the fireplace, drinking in the warmth on our skin.

I couldn't help it; my eyes kept straying back to Evelyn. Dad and Dr. M had the map spread out again on a table across the lobby; they had found two rickety chairs to sit on. Dad's chair was uneven. That or it was the floor. Every time he shifted his weight, the opposite leg clanked down against the floorboards with a hollow thud.

"When they realize we aren't back, once it's been fully dark for a bit, they'll start to worry. They'll call someone... the police." I strained to listen for Dad's response.

"Yeah, and what'll they do? Probably nothing at first. Not until morning. I don't envision a team out here combing the woods for a hunting group that's been missing for less than a few hours."

Dr. M sighed deeply. "Okay, go over the route and draw it in this time. Might as well." They were trying to plot out what Dad thought would be the fastest route back to civilization, taking in the terrain the best they could tell from the map.

My eyes wandered back over to Evelyn again. She had thought to bring her book along, in case she got bored while we were hunting. She had pulled it out of the bag she'd carried, slung over one shoulder, and sat cross-legged, reading by firelight. It wasn't fully dark yet but getting close. I peered over at the nearest windows: squares of black. I pictured someone standing there, watching us, and shuddered slightly, turning back to the fire. It was more comforting to stare into the flames than out into the void.

I attempted to watch Evelyn without being obvious. She had taken off her coat and the sweater she had on underneath. She wore only a thin V-neck t-shirt. The neckline dipped dangerously low, revealing the swelling curves of her cleavage, her pale skin in between coated in the finest down of little golden hairs, just visible in the firelight. I swallowed dryly, clearing my throat, and coughed, choking a little.

She turned to look sharply over at me, and I looked away immediately. *Great.* That wasn't suspicious at all. I grabbed my water bottle, taking a tiny sip. That was all I would allow myself. We needed water, having walked miles today, but we had to conserve what little we had.

"Oh god," Evelyn said, tipping up the book and placing a hand over the cover. "You saw it, didn't you?" She grinned over at me, her expression hard to read. It was a sort of devious smile, but she looked embarrassed at the same time. I grinned back, and before she could react, I lunged forward, grabbing the book by the corner. Not expecting it, she hadn't been holding on tight enough, and it flew easily out of her hands.

"Teddy!" She exclaimed, "Give it back!" And I scrambled away from her as she lunged back towards me, hand outstretched, reaching for the book. I was on my feet in seconds, and moving away from her, holding it aloft as she raced over to me and jumped to grab it. She wasn't anywhere near tall enough. I turned and jogged up the stairs.

Dad had given the stairs and the second floor the all clear, warning us to tread carefully. He hadn't bothered to search the third floor well and asked us to avoid it.

I heard him call out, "Kids!" In a tired sort of voice, that told me he didn't really care all that much. I kept going, leaping over a hole in the floorboards, and almost turning into the first room. I continued to the second room, it contained an ancient narrow bed and bedside dresser. I moved around to the far side of the bed, leaving behind a trail of tracks of bare floor revealed under the thick layer of dust.

I stood in front of the window, holding the book up close as I peered at it in the faint light, scanning the jacket description. Creaking footsteps echoed out in the hall, and Evelyn appeared in the doorframe. She stepped swiftly over towards the bed. "Ooh." I grinned. "Listen to this: 'The ruggedly handsome Sheriff Jack Hurdley is hot on the case...'"

"Shut up Teddy, for real." Evelyn started laughing as she began to move around the bed. "Give it back to me."

I still held her place, my thumb tucked between the pages. I flipped the book open and skimmed the top of the page. "Oh, it gets better; 'I can't give up, Grace. Not until I've tracked down every last one of them. What they did is unconscionable; I won't stand for it. But I'll come back. I won't be able to stay away.'" I snorted. "What is this? Some cheesy Western?" I flipped over to the front cover. It depicted a man in a cowboy hat, wearing a gold star, holding a woman in a blue dress, his lips hovered over hers. "*Beneath the North Star*?" I read the title out loud. "Is this some corny Western Romance novel Ev? You've got to be kidding me." I chuckled again and flipped back to the page.

"Shut up!" Evelyn reached me and swatted at my arm. I lifted the book higher, turning to the side, so she missed when she grabbed for it. "You're such a jerk Teddy, I knew you'd make fun of me." Her cheeks were flushed bright red in the dusk. "So it's not Shakespeare." She said 'Shakespeare' in an exaggerated, pretentious voice. "Do you really think it's any different?"

"Than Shakespeare?" I asked, eyebrows raised. "Yeah, Ev, I do."

"That's because you're a literary snob. Almost all of Shakespeare's plays are love stories, and they were considered pretty risqué for their time." She crossed her arms over her chest, jaw raised in a stubborn tilt.

"Okay." I laughed. "Point taken. But listen to this." I cleared my throat, continuing to read in my best impression of a southern accent. "'I promise I'll do everything I can to find my way back to you, Grace, once I've made the frontier a safer place. You're the only reason I can keep going, keep fighting.'" I snorted. "So that's your type, huh? You like lone ranger heroes, who carry six-shooters, Ev?"

She sneered at me. "No, Teddy." She tilted her head to the side. "I prefer villains. You know, assholes, like you," she said, her voice dripping with sarcasm. My cheeks burned. She rolled her eyes and lunged again.

But I was too quick, turning away from her, twisting in the opposite direction, as I continued reading. "'I know it's risky, and there's a chance I won't make it back, Grace, but this is something I have to do. If I don't make it back-'" I laughed, eyes jumping further down the page as Evelyn pulled my arm down low, causing me to lose my spot. "'You're a beauty, Grace, a beauty I just can't seem to forget.' Oh, give me a break. Do girls really fall for this drivel?" I snickered, as she finally managed to snatch the book out of my hands. "Even I can do better than that."

"Oh yeah?" Evelyn's lips were pressed in a tight line as she glared up at me. "I'd love to see you try," she snapped. Her nostrils flared slightly with each breath, and I could tell, even in the dim, fading light, that her cheeks were bright red. Two splotches of flame spread over her pale as porcelain skin. I realized then she wasn't laughing anymore. Didn't think it was funny. That I'd actually managed to make her upset. I watched her, taking in the rise and fall of her chest. She was still painfully beautiful, even when she was mad. And I wanted her. Wanted her more than I'd ever wanted anything.

I could feel my chest filling with a sort of hollow recklessness. Like a balloon inflating rapidly, growing out of control. I knew I should just stop; knew I should apologize and leave her be. I didn't know whether it was the darkness surrounding us, the moonlight shining on her face, throwing her features into stark black and white shadows, or the sight of her flustered, worked up and angry. But I felt, suddenly, like doing something risky myself. I took a step towards her.

"Yeah? Would you?" I asked, sliding closer to her, my voice pitched low.

She snorted, rolling her eyes slightly. "Yes, Teddy. Why don't you go ahead, be my guest." She swept an arm in front of her. "Make me swoon, just like Grace." Correction, she wasn't just mad, she was furious. She crossed her arms back over her chest, book still in hand, tucked under one arm. She glared up at me.

I shrugged, smirking a little. "Sure, why not? I'll give it a shot." Like it was no big deal.

She just stood there, staring me down, eyes narrowed. I didn't look away, meeting her gaze. I reached her, and tucking a finger under her chin, I tilted her face gently upwards, towards mine, until her eyes widened slightly, and she stilled.

My heart pounded loudly in my chest, and I couldn't believe I was about to do this, but before I could think better of it, I opened my mouth and let the words I'd formulated in my mind earlier, the ones I couldn't seem to say, come spilling out.

"How about this," I said quietly, pausing for a moment. My heart was in my throat now, and I knew with certainty that this was either one of the dumbest or one of the smartest things I'd ever done. Either way it was too late to stop now.

"Your eyes are like two green pools I could drown in." I studied them for a moment, then ran a finger up to trace the curve of her full lips. Evelyn was frozen, giving away not the slightest hint of the effect of my words so far. "And your lips... I could try to write a poem about your lips, or a song." I grinned slightly, "But it would never end, and the words wouldn't come."

My eyes dropped to her lips, and she swallowed, her eyes dipping to mine, as I continued to trace hers, brushing her plump bottom lip with the pad of my thumb. "So, I'll just tell you how I could listen to you talk, forever, just to watch them move."

My eyes found hers again, my voice dropping lower. "And how I bet kissing you, would feel like dying, but I'd gladly do it over, and over again."

Only her pupils moved, widening in the swiftly darkening night, as a cloud blew over the moon, shrouding us in near complete darkness. I paused, my heart hammering louder, until I was sure she could hear it. "And let me tell you something about heroes and villains, Evelyn." My voice dropped to a whisper, "A hero, would give you up and ride off into the sunset to save the world. But a villain? A villain would give up the world for you. He would lay it at your feet. Would let it burn, just for a chance to hold you."

She finally moved, closing her eyes, her long eyelashes shuttering like curtains as I leaned in to kiss her. And I was right, kissing her did feel a little like dying. Full of longing and want. Desperation and need. Sharp and real and exquisite, to the point of pain. My whole body was on fire by the time she pulled away from me.

And I knew at that moment that the little line I'd crafted was true. Because I'd burn the entire world, burn everything, to have her.

"Where are you guys?" Katie's voice called out from the hallway, just outside the room, and we both jumped, Evelyn gasping slightly, mouth still centimeters from mine. The sound sent shivers up my spine, and I nearly moaned, pulling her waist closer to me involuntarily, one hand still on her hip, the other cupped around her arm. I could feel the goosebumps, little raised pebbles on her skin. I wanted to pull her back in, kiss her again. But I let her go as she pulled further away from me, stepping back out of my arms completely before Katie entered the room.

Damn it Katie. I groaned internally, cursing the interruption. She seemed to have a knack for popping up at precisely the wrong moment.

"What are you guys doing?" Katie asked, her voice void of suspicion, filled only with curiosity. Evelyn just stared at her, her chest still rising and falling rapidly, an odd expression on her face, like she was too rattled to speak.

"Nothing," I managed to mutter, hoarsely. "I was just making fun of Ev." I gestured towards the book, still clutched in her hands. "I was teasing her about her book." I shrugged and smiled reassuringly at Katie as her brows wrinkled, the start of a frown forming on her lips. "Just joking around, Katie." I turned to the window, pulling the curtain further aside with one hand, trying to calm my own breathing, steady my heart rate. I peered out at the light cover of snow on the ground. Large, puffy snowflakes had started to fall again. I scanned the darkness at the edge of the forest. The woods around us remained silent.

"It's cold up here," Katie murmured. "I hope Dad is okay. He's out there... somewhere, in the cold." I felt a stab of guilt pierce my chest at her words. It was as though she'd thrown a bucket of ice water over me, stamping out the desire still coursing through my body in an instant. I'd somehow managed to momentarily forget what was happening; I was up here, making up soppy lines and kissing Evelyn, while Katie and Ryan's Dad was lost out there somewhere in the cold.

Lost, or worse, dead. A voice in the back of my mind murmured. That intrusive little voice that liked to speak the truths I didn't want to hear.

I sighed and turned around. "Oh Katie," Evelyn murmured, beating me to it. She moved around the bed, and took Katie's hands in hers, then pulled her in for a hug. "It's going to be okay. It'll all work out somehow."

"But what do you think happened, Teddy?" Katie sniffed, over Evelyn's shoulders, and I could hear the unshed tears building behind her voice. "That had to have been my Dad. If not... if not... what happened to him?" Her lips started trembling and the floodgates burst open, tears streaming down her cheeks. She wiped them away, silently, as Evelyn murmured comforting things, patting her on the back. We stood there for several minutes, until she began to calm down. I stared out the window, useless, not answering her question.

How could I? I didn't have any answers, any explanations. I thought back to the cryptid book that Dr. Carter had brought to the house. Was it true that there was something, or someone, in these woods, that could shape-shift? Take on the characteristics of another person? I didn't want to say the word skin-walker, not even to myself, in my own head. But there had been a general theme to a lot of the stories in the book, and the stories Mr. Johnson had told us.

Nearly all of them hinted at someone, an entity, or a person, living out in the woods, involved in people disappearing. Maybe there was a more rational explanation. Maybe something happened to people who came out here. Maybe it *was* Dr. Carter, but he had been *changed*. Affected, somehow. My mind raced, thinking over everything I had read, everything I had heard. Cataloging and categorizing. I didn't have the answers, yet. But I had some information, and some was better than none. Maybe something I had heard, or read, would help us figure this out.

Evelyn and Katie were calling me to head back downstairs with them. I turned and followed them silently back down the staircase to the lobby. Dad and Dr. M had piled up old rugs and spread out our sleeping bags on the ground, making them as big as possible. We wouldn't have blankets to cover us, not unless we wanted to use the moldy decrepit blankets off of the filthy hotel beds, but the fire would keep us warm enough. Thanks to our earlier efforts, we still had a pile of firewood to go through.

We split up our sandwiches, each of us eating half and saving the rest for the morning. We had a few bags of chips to go around.

There were some protein bars left over that we chose to save. I'm sure none of us felt full, or satisfied, but it would have to do, for now.

We settled down to try to get some rest, at Dad and Dr. M's insistence. I used my coat bundled up as a pillow, and Evelyn did the same. Katie attempted to lay down as well. Ryan lay down to sleep with his rifle lying next to him on one side, and the baseball bat on the other.

After fifteen minutes or so of Katie flopping around restlessly, she sighed and sat up. "I can't sleep," she moaned. She stood and walked away from the fire, shucking her coat over her shoulders as she went. She grabbed the flashlight off the table, and switched it on, shining it out the windows as she walked the length of the lobby.

"Katie," Dad called out, "please try to conserve battery life." Katie sighed loudly, but she switched the flashlight off with a click. I realized, when I could hear it, that I had left my hearing aids in. Normally I'd take them off at night, but I didn't like the thought of taking them off here. I'd rather have every chance of hearing if someone, or something, were to try to sneak up on us in our sleep.

I propped myself up on one elbow to see Dad was still sitting, eyes heavy, but open, over by the fire. He had set a chair down, facing out towards the windows. His shotgun lay across his lap. Clearly, he wasn't about to let anyone sneak up on us. He saw me watching him and nodded to me. "Get some sleep, Teddy," he murmured. I nodded back and laid back down.

If I woke up in a bit, I'd offer to take a watch. I wasn't a particularly heavy sleeper, and had a feeling I wouldn't sleep well here. The cold from the hard floorboards was already seeping through the layers of rug and sleeping bag to chill my skin. I gazed over in Evelyn's direction as my eyes closed and opened, closed and opened. She appeared to be already asleep, or on her way there. She was lying on her side, facing me, and her eyes remained closed, from what I could tell in the flickering firelight. Her romance novel lay near her hands.

I did my best not to think about the flash of her eyes when she was angry, the feel of her lips on mine, the feeling of her tongue in my mouth, my hand on her waist. I sighed deeply, flipping over on my back to stare at the ceiling. It was going to be a long night.

12

— · —

I woke to the sound of screaming. Katie cried out in a desperate
voice, "It's Dad, Ryan! It's Dad!" She was pounding on the
window with one fist, the flashlight in her hand shining on the
glass, a glare, reflected back to me.

"Katie, hang on sweetie." I heard Dad say, his voice gruff as he
struggled to sit up from his spot on the floor. I was half-propped
up on my elbows, heart pounding in my chest. My eyes wouldn't
open fully; I was struggling to orient myself again to where I was,
but it was coming back to me.

Katie grabbed the spare shotgun from where it sat propped
up by the front door, and before I knew what was happening, she
had pulled the door open and disappeared into the night. I gaped,
staring at the door as it slowly continued to swing open, until it
banged into the wall and bounced back.

Dad and Dr. M were on their feet, Dr. M shrugging into his
coat, rifle already in hand. "Katie!" he called out and disappeared
after her through the door. Dad was making quick work of following him. He still had his coat on, but he messed with something on
the ground, probably grabbing more shells.

He stood up with his shotgun in his hand, slung it over his shoulder, and moved quickly over to me, glancing towards the door. "Teddy." He grasped me on the shoulder, crouching down as I struggled to sit up. "The map is on the table; I marked the best route out. You have the compass." He glanced towards the door again. I heard shouts echoing outside. "If we don't come back, you get out of here. You wait until daylight and then you go, immediately. You don't stop. You get them out. You get yourself out." He glanced over towards Ryan and Evelyn and then back to me.

"Dad..." I began to protest, my heart hammering in my throat. *What was he talking about?*

"Teddy, listen to me, son." He grabbed my chin, staring into my eyes. "You remember what I taught you, and you get yourself out. You do whatever you have to, Teddy. Do you understand me?" He was yelling now, liquid lining his eyes in the firelight. "Do you understand me?"

"Yes!" I cried back at him. He nodded once, leaning forward, he kissed me on the top of the head, and then he was gone, sprinting through the door, out into the night.

I scrambled to my feet, fumbling on the ground for my shotgun. I didn't bother with my coat. I ran after him. I barely registered Evelyn calling out my name. I was out on the porch, eyes scanning the darkness. I could see nothing; no sign of any of them. "Damn it," I cursed, stepping down off the porch onto the snow. I scanned the ground the best I could, waiting impatiently for a cloud that was passing swiftly across the moon above.

I thought I could see footprints in the snow, and when the cloud finally cleared and the moonlight shone down fully again, I saw that I was right. A trail of footprints led off to my left, towards the woods. Two sets of intermingled footprints further to the right, crisscrossing over each other, eventually turning towards the woods as well.

I could follow them only that far. Katie had run off with the only flashlight. It wouldn't be so easy to follow their trail in the woods, under the shadows of the trees, without one. It would be slow going, but it was doable. Besides, how far could they have gone?

I strained, listening for their voices calling on the wind, but there was only the cold echoing howl of the wind over snow and the rustling of trees, their limbs swaying, branches creaking and groaning.

Evelyn slammed into my back from behind, and I jumped slightly. "Teddy, no." She grabbed onto my arm, pulling me back towards the house. I refused to move, planting my feet and scanning the treeline for any sign of them.

"I'm going after them, Ev. They can't have gotten that far." I strained again to listen. "Can you hear anything?"

I turned to look at her, and saw fear there, her green eyes wide as she scanned the wall of black in the forest beyond. "No, Teddy." She paused for a moment, listening. "I can't hear anything. And you can't go after them. It's pitch black out here. You have to come back inside."

I shook my head, turning back to the woods. She tugged on my arm again, harder. "I'll track them." I indicated the footprints in the snow, "Follow their footprints."

"You can't hope to do that in the dark," she hissed at me. "Teddy, be serious. We need to get back inside." I frowned, scanning the treeline again. I didn't want to hear it. I needed to follow my dad, find him, quickly, before they got too far away.

He didn't have the map. Or the compass, I remembered, with a stab of real fear now. They would get turned around out in the woods, trying to follow Katie. They had almost no hope of making their way back here, blind in the dark, not even the sun to help orient them. *What was he thinking?*

Evelyn tugged harder now on my arm, her hands sliding up to my bicep. "Teddy, please, let's go, now. They'll find her and head back soon."

"Evelyn." I turned, snapping at her now, "I'm not leaving them out here. It's dark. Dad doesn't have the map, or the compass." I pointed up to the sky. "There's no sun right now," I sputtered, "how do you think they're going to find their way back here, exactly?" I ran a hand through my hair, turning away from her, back towards the woods. I could feel tears start to gather in my eyes, as the reality of the situation fully sank in. "They're screwed," I murmured.

We heard it, then. The howling, starting up again. It was just as terrifying and bone-chilling as it had been before, if not more so now, out here in the dark. "No," I murmured, "no, no..." The howling was growing louder, as more took up the call. How many of them were there? How many... We both jumped as a barrage of shotgun blasts went off. A rifle cracking in tandem in the distance. Evelyn let out a strangled sob, as I tried desperately to count the number of rounds, ears straining, waiting for more.

"Teddy," Evelyn cried out, tugging me hard enough that I fell a half step backwards. I could hear the panic and fear, her voice dripping with it. "Teddy, please, please." She yelped, as another howl rang out into the night, much closer this time. Far too close.

I turned to the left, scanning the treeline in the direction of the howling that trailed off into a keening whine. Evelyn stepped in front of me, putting herself in my line of sight. Her hand against my cheek was ice cold, as she turned my head, titling it down, forcing me to look at her.

"Teddy, look at me," she murmured, her eyes wide and panicked, face white as bone in the moonlight. "You need to come inside with me, now." I looked back at the woods, wanting to run, to search for them. "Teddy, listen." She pulled me back to her. "Listen, if you care about me, at all, you need to come with me, now." Her voice steadied, gaining confidence as she spoke. "Let's go. Now. Move it." It was an order, not a request. I brought my gaze back to the edge of the woods one more time. *You get them out. You get yourself out. You get them out.*

I swallowed, my throat dry, and nodded. She let go of my face, her hands dropping to mine. She took my hand in both of hers, and she led me back towards the porch, never taking her eyes off of me, keeping my focus on her.

I followed her, numbly. Numb with cold and dread. My Dad was out there, in those woods. And I had failed him.

She pulled me inside with the power of her eyes on mine until I stood back in the lobby of the dilapidated hotel, and she slammed the door shut behind us.

13

—·—

E velyn dragged one of the chairs over to the door, and propped
it under the handle, wedging it between the handle and floor.
I stared numbly at the fire. Then at Ryan.

He sat in the chair near the fireplace. The one Dad had sat
watch in as I fell asleep. He had his rifle slung across his lap, the
baseball bat standing upright next to him, the handle in his hand.
He stared back at me, his face almost expressionless. Watchful.
Guarded.

I said nothing to him, turning and walking over to the stairs. I
moved up them swiftly, not really caring if I stepped in a hole, and
made it to the top. I moved down the hallway to a room that faced
the woods where they had disappeared. I stood in the window for
a long time, watching and waiting.

But there was no sign of them. Not a hint of movement. Nothing crossed the expanse of white below, between us and the woods.
And though the howling went on, the mournful cries became
fewer, and farther between, until they stopped altogether.

I stood there, elbows locked, hands pressed down on the window frame, putting my weight on my arms, tilting forward, then

back, forward, then back again. I could feel the edge of panic, hovering over me. The hot burn of fear. Of rage, and grief, billowing in my chest. *You get them out. Get them out. Get them out.*

But this couldn't be real. Couldn't be happening. Dad would walk out of the woods. He'd walk out at any moment. I waited. I held off the panic. It was like putting the fear on hold. It wasn't gone. It wasn't going anywhere. Not until I let it out. But it would wait. For now, at least. And Dad would walk out of the woods. *Yeah*, the little voice whispered, *but will it really be him?*

Eventually I gave up and went back downstairs. I found Evelyn and Ryan sitting by the fire, fresh branches thrown on. They had been murmuring together as I moved down the staircase. But they stopped talking abruptly when they saw me standing at the base of the stairs.

Ryan looked at Evelyn, then back at me. "Teddy," he spoke up, "why don't you get some sleep? We need to rest. Get ready for tomorrow."

I stared at him, eyes narrowing. Why was he so calm? I shook my head, looking over at Evelyn. Her eyes and nose were red. Like she'd been crying. Crying with *him* there to comfort her. I felt my hands clench into fists.

I moved over to the little table and took a seat. "You two get some rest. I'll take first watch."

I insisted, despite Ryan's protests. I knew one thing for sure; I wouldn't be sleeping again tonight.

14

— • —

The knocking started about an hour later. I sat in the chair, one hand resting on my shotgun on the table. I watched them sleep.

Watched as Evelyn's chest rose and fell, her expression peaceful. I watched Ryan as he twitched, tossing and turning in his sleep. Although unconscious, he looked as restless as I felt.

I was on high alert, my nerves already taut, but even still, I jumped, startled by that first knock.

Bang-bang-bang. A set of three, just like back at the rental house. I stood as Evelyn and Ryan began to stir, stretching and blinking awake.

I stalked over to the nearest window, peering out through the dirty, fogged glass, scanning the ground below. Another knock came farther away to my left. I followed along the wall, peeking through each window as I went. The sky was more overcast now, and the wind had picked up. Clouds rolling over the moon in rapid succession. I peered at the ground during gaps in the cloud cover because unlike last night, tonight, there was a fresh blanket of snow, and that meant footprints.

I moved from one window to the next, following the deliberate knocking, slow and even, and taunting. Even with the moonlight, it was hard to see much beyond the edge of the wrap-around porch, especially with the snow steadily falling. But I could see what were clearly tracks, elongated, human-like prints, just beyond the porch in this section, and the layer of snow that had been disturbed on the porch railing, where it had climbed over.

"Teddy, don't," Evelyn called out from somewhere behind me. The intervals between knocks were getting shorter. I made it to the next window just as another knock sounded and managed to catch a glimpse of something moving out in the dark. A limb? A pale glint in the moonlight, there for a fraction of a second.

I sprinted for the next window, and reaching it, I set my shotgun down against the wall, and shoved the window open as quickly as I could. It moved with a reluctant squeaky groan, the first knock sounding as the window ground to a halt. I grabbed my shotgun, the figure pausing, and I could see well enough to know it wasn't a person. Wasn't human. It wasn't Dad, or Dr. Montgomery, or Katie... It was much too tall, with a stooped back and long white limbs. Its back was to me. I took aim and shot.

The pale figure moved so fast. Too fast. Seeming to sense the shot coming, it ducked down low, and flung itself over the railing, disappearing into the night.

The bang of the shotgun blast was far too loud, reverberating inside the room. My hearing aids, trying to block it, dropped the volume down for several seconds afterwards, and all I could hear was a high-pitched ringing. I couldn't tell for a few seconds if it was coming from inside my own head or if it was just feedback.

The world around me came back into focus, like a radio being turned slowly back up, as the ringing trailed off and ambient sound flooded back in. I could hear Evelyn and Ryan now. Ryan had grabbed his rifle and was over to my left, a few windows down. He had shoved open his window too and was hanging half out of it, swinging the end of the rifle back and forth.

Evelyn was crying out from across the lobby, "They're over here now!" Her voice thick with fear.

I met Ryan's eyes as he turned, and he nodded once to me. We moved over to the far side of the lobby; he fell in behind me as we moved to the right, sidling up against the wall, shuffling with our knees bent. I paused to peek up at each window we passed, peering out into the darkness. Nothing at the first three.

We made it over to the corner. Evelyn was crouched down on the sleeping bags, her rifle clutched against her chest, wide eyes darting back and forth.

I stilled, listening, waiting for the next knock. Nothing. I turned and motioned to Ryan, pointing at the farthest window and waving him on. He moved quickly to the far window, and I moved to the first window. We waited, still, for the knocking to start up again. It came from my left, closer to Ryan, and he stood and shoved his window open.

I heard a hissing sound as he aimed and took a shot; he was screaming something.

I heard scrambling out on the porch as I shoved my window open too. Evelyn was screaming now behind us. I caught a glimpse of something white disappearing over the railing and tracked it as far as I could. I couldn't count how many limbs it had. It shot through the blanket of falling snow, snowflakes swirling briefly in its wake, and then it was gone.

"Holy shit," Ryan said, turning and slamming his back into the wall as he slid down to the floor, chest heaving. "It looked right at me." He gasped a breath. "Fuck."

"I don't think they can come inside," I said slowly, still peering out the window after it.

"Why are you assuming that?" Ryan asked, brows wrinkled as he frowned over at me.

"Why the knocking, otherwise? You're telling me those things aren't strong enough to break the door down if they wanted to?" I nodded at the door, the chair still shoved under the handle. "We opened the windows multiple times, and they didn't try to come in. The knocking... I think they're trying to lure us to come out."

"What did it look like?" Evelyn whispered.

I watched Ryan as he thought for a moment. "Human, but... not."

I nodded, turning to Evelyn. "They're tall, pale skin, long white limbs. I didn't see its face."

Evelyn was silent for a moment. "What are they?" Her voice still a whisper.

I shook my head, and so did Ryan. "I don't know," I said slowly. "Skin-walkers? Maybe?" I shrugged. "But whatever they are, I think it's pretty safe to assume they're what's responsible for all the people that have gone missing out here."

We were all quiet for several moments, then Evelyn spoke again. "What do we do now?" she asked, looking up at me with wide, solemn eyes.

I looked over at the map, still spread out on the table, and nodded at it. "We wait until daylight. Sunrise. We drink the water we have, eat something. We'll refill our water bottles in the stream. It's water flowing down from the mountains, it should be clean enough. Safe enough to drink. We'll need all of our strength."

I looked back and forth between them. "We're going to hike out of here tomorrow. It's far, but it's doable. We don't stop. We move as fast as we can. We'll be fighting against the daylight. Everything indicates it's more dangerous at night. Although, I'm not positive they won't be... active during the day, it does seem like there are more of them at night. Maybe they don't like the sun."

Evelyn thought for a moment. "That's what you think he was?" she asked me, her voice tentative. "Dr. Carter." She looked over at Ryan from beneath her brows. He looked down at his feet. "Maybe that's it."

"What do you mean?" I asked, brows wrinkled in confusion.

"Maybe that's how they can move around, during the day, I mean. Maybe they have to be... changed." I thought about it for a long moment, and realized she was probably right. That made sense. Well, at least as much sense as any of this could make. The beings we just saw, that came out knocking at night, maybe that was their true form. Maybe they needed a host during the day.

I frowned. "That does make sense. But..." I waited for my thoughts to formulate fully. "We don't know how any of this works. Are we... are humans like... the host? Are they inside of the person? Or do they... do they really take..." my voice trailed off. "Take their skins? Do they take part of us and turn into us somehow?" I couldn't believe the shit I was saying. This felt like a nightmare that I couldn't pull myself out of. None of this could be real, it was insane. But that thing, outside, *that* had been real. There was no denying it.

Evelyn sighed deeply. "I don't know. But either way, the plan is a good one. We need to get out of here. Call for help, try to find the others."

I looked over at her, and Ryan and I met each other's gaze briefly. I wasn't so sure there would be anyone out there to rescue, and I could tell from his grim expression that he wasn't either.

But I nodded to Evelyn. "We'll have one day. To make it out. We'll have to make every minute count."

I sat awake for quite some time after they lay back down to try to sleep, studying the map by the moonlight. I could feel it coming, now that the adrenaline had worn off, and I wasn't sure I could delay it any longer. I'd made the rounds and shut all of the windows, making sure they were latched, but each shuttered window seemed to stare back at me, like dark eyes, opening into a sea of black.

I tried to focus on breathing, keeping my breaths calm and even and deep. I repeated *The Litany Against Fear,* over and over in my head, like a mantra. The familiar words beat out a rhythm in my brain. It had worked before, many times. I might not always be able to prevent an attack, but I could try to shorten it. I'd learned that, eventually. To accept it, stop fighting it. I focused on trying to keep the panic at a minimum and shortening the length of it. I couldn't stop it entirely.

I thought about going upstairs so they didn't hear me, but I didn't want to risk leaving Evelyn. I couldn't sit still, though, and after a while I got up and paced, sticking to the far side of the room.

Evelyn sat up several minutes later, combing the room for me. I wasn't sure she had ever really gone back to sleep. My body was trembling by then, minute shivers, my teeth chattering slightly. This was a bad one

She seemed to sense my distress as she moved closer to me in the dark. The fire has died down, reduced to orange glowing coals. I should have put more wood on to keep them warm while they slept.

"Oh, Teddy," she murmured, moving closer to me and sighing. I just shook my head at her, trying to stop my teeth chattering.

"I'm fine. It's fine. Go back to sleep." My voice came out funny, syllables falling in an odd, clipped sort of way as I tried to speak through my clenched jaw.

"No, you're clearly not fine." She shook her head at me.

"I will be," I replied. "I always am. It just takes a while. I just have to get through it. It's just..." I trailed off, laughing a little, "it's so lame." My stomach twisted and I took a deep breath through my nose. I refused to puke in front of her but when the attacks were bad, I had to fight not to vomit.

"It's not lame, Teddy," she began, but I cut her off.

"Yes, it is. Literally nothing is happening right now, and my body... my body feels like I'm being chased by a fucking lion. It doesn't make any sense." I laughed darkly. "Tell me why I was fine earlier? I was able to stay calm. But now that it's over? Now that nothing's happening? I can't fucking deal. I'm terrified. Of... nothing?" I shook my head in disgust. "So yeah, it's dumb."

She looked at me for a long time without saying anything. "Emotions aren't dumb, Teddy. They aren't necessarily logical, either." She paused. "Maybe your body is letting you feel everything now, after the fact. Once you're safe? I don't know," she said, moving closer to me. I was shaking harder now, after the effort of speaking. She slipped her hand into mine and squeezed it. I squeezed back, probably harder than I should have, then relaxed my grip. "Either way, it's not stupid. And you don't need to be embarrassed. Not around me."

I looked away from her, shaking my head. I didn't say anything for a bit. She squeezed my hand tighter, and I tried to take deep breaths. Tried to slow down. I hated it. Hated that I couldn't control it. Couldn't make it stop. And maybe that was the worst part. The lack of control.

"That's it Teddy, just squeeze my hand. Take deep breaths." She nodded, trying to encourage me, but it wasn't working. I wanted to crawl out of my own skin. I nodded, trying harder to breathe evenly, but the panic just kept coming, kept rising.

"What do you do normally, like at home?" she asked, curious.

"Um," I replied, my teeth still chattering. I let them. Sometimes the shaking helped release the energy somehow, letting me get through it faster. "I ah... listen to music sometimes, familiar songs will help me. Or I..." I flushed a little, "Repeat certain things, like sayings or..." I shrugged. "You remember *The Litany Against Fear*, from *Dune*?" She nodded. "Well, I say that sometimes. That helps. Moving helps." I shrugged. "I think about the books I've read. Like, the characters... remind myself what they were able to do." I felt myself flushing deeply now. "I know they're just stupid stories, but, I dunno..." I trailed off. "I try different things."

Evelyn nodded, smiling a bit in the dark. "They aren't just stupid stories, Teddy." She shook her head. "That's the whole point, really. The whole point of reading. The whole point of telling stories. They give us hope. Make us feel less alone, braver, even when we have no reason to be." She smiled again. "I do the same thing, sometimes. When I'm sad or upset. Picture myself in a story, or, think of one of my favorite characters, and what they would do." She shrugged. "I don't think that sounds stupid at all."

For some reason I felt myself suddenly overwhelmed with a rush of emotion, practically tearing up at her words, and I was grateful for the darkness. I guess it was because she understood. We stood there silently for a moment, while I shivered.

"I like that... *The Litany Against Fear.*" She looked thoughtful. "What's that famous saying? You have nothing to fear, but fear itself?" She smiled at me in the dark. "It always makes me think of that. How true that is. Fear, feeling afraid, is almost always worse than the thing itself. You know?" I nodded, taking a deep breath. I could feel the shivering slowing down a bit now. Evelyn grimaced slightly. "Although, I guess that's not... always, the case. Necessarily." She frowned, gazing out the window, into the black and whatever lurked beyond.

She turned back suddenly. "Music helps?" she asked, grinning at me. I nodded briskly. "Okay," she sighed. "But you can't judge me. Okay?"

"Okay..." I said slowly, frowning in confusion.

"Come on," she said, turning and leading me by the hand over to the dilapidated couch. She sat down and pulled me onto the couch next to her. She tucked my hand in hers, squeezing tight. I squeezed back, watching her, trying to keep the unrelenting panic down.

She took a deep breath, and she started to sing. I wasn't expecting it, somehow. Her voice was sweet and clear, but with a huskiness to it, on those low notes. I was so surprised and distracted that I realized with a shock a minute or two later, that I'd stopped trembling. My teeth had stopped chattering, and she had distracted me so completely, that it seemed to be actually working.

She sang a sad, slow song, and I thought I recognized the lyrics from somewhere. They were familiar, although I couldn't name the song. I stared at her, her green eyes closing and opening as she sang. She didn't really look at me. If she did, she wasn't seeing me. She had an amazing voice. Absolutely beautiful. I felt my hand relax in hers. She sang for maybe five minutes, maybe more. Moving swiftly on to another song when the first one ended.

When she stopped, I was calmer. Calm enough. I could feel myself coming out of it. She smiled at me, and leaned forward, cupping the side of my face in her hand. "Another saying, I remember the gist of; being brave isn't the absence of fear, it's feeling afraid, and facing your fear. Doing it anyway."

"That was... beautiful, Evelyn. You have an amazing voice. Thank you," I added. My chest filled with warmth at her smile. I had no idea she could sing like that, and I felt honored she shared it with me.

"Thanks, Teddy." She smiled warmly back at me. Her hand was cold on my cheek. "Did it work?"

"Yeah." I grinned. "I think it did, it was very distracting."

"Good." She grinned back at me. I could see her, thinking for a moment. Then she leaned forward and whispered. "I just thought of something else that might distract you."

Her lips on mine felt like heaven. And she was right.

15

—•—

We were ready at dawn. I made sure of it. Evelyn went to sleep after our late-night kiss. Of course I wanted it to turn into more, but it wasn't really the right timing. Or the right place. I refused to sleep. She insisted, and we argued for a bit, but ultimately, she gave in and went to lay down. I'd gotten four hours of sleep before everything went down. Maybe five. I'd suffered from insomnia often enough to know I could function pretty well on that amount of sleep. It would be enough.

I sat watching and woke them at first light. We drank the water we had and planned to stop at the stream on our way out.

We ate the rest of our sandwiches, saving the protein bars for lunch. We agreed we would stop only as needed to go to the bathroom, but otherwise we would need to be constantly moving, even if at a slow pace.

I studied the map for what felt like the hundredth time, tracing the pencil marks Dad had left behind. I estimated the hike out would be at least 10 miles, probably closer to 12. Assuming we were able to walk at a pace of at least two miles per hour, it should only take us five or six hours to make it to Mount Snow. It wasn't much farther from there to our rental houses. We should, in theory, have plenty of daylight, assuming nothing went horribly wrong.

We set out in silence. The sun was bright already, although low in the sky and thankfully the sky looked fairly cloudless at the moment. I was hopeful the sun would add at least a little warmth, and we would be moving constantly, which should help us keep warm as well.

But that first step out of the relative warmth of the hotel into the cold was still jolting. The sets of footprints surrounding the hotel, even more so. In the light of day, without falling snow obscuring our vision, we could see tracks visible... everywhere. They surrounded the hotel, intersecting sets of tracks creating a jumbled mess in the pristine snow. The tracks led away from the hotel and back into the woods, in the direction we were headed.

"Jesus H. Christ..." Evelyn murmured; jaw dropped slightly open as she stared at the tracks. "How many of them are there?" She turned to look at me, eyes wide.

I could only shake my head. "I don't think we want to know." I patted my hand reassuringly against my chest, feeling the map folded there, and the compass. "Our route will take us near enough to where we parked the cars, that I think it's worth stopping there first. We have more shells in the gun case..." I trailed off, thinking for a moment. "Besides, doesn't it make sense to stop there and just make sure there isn't someone else there? What if there's a group there with a working car? We might get lucky and be able to get a ride out of here."

"You don't think it would be much out of our way?" Evelyn asked, biting her bottom lip. I'd thought about it last night, while she and Ryan slept. It was a slight risk, adding the extra time to jog south a bit and back up, but the potential reward seemed to outweigh the risk. Not to mention the comfort more ammo would bring.

I nodded. "I think it will add a bit of time, but not much. It'll take us south a bit farther out of our way, but I think it's worth the risk." I looked over at Ryan, trying to gauge his reaction. "What do you think?" I asked them both.

Evelyn thought for a moment, then nodded in agreement. We both turned to Ryan. He licked his lips and looked over at the edge of the forest. "Yeah..." he murmured after a moment. "It seems like a good idea. Let's do it."

"Okay." I nodded. "That's settled. Let's get going; we'll head for the stream we crossed on the way in." I pulled the compass out of my coat, and held it aloft, getting my bearings. "This way," I called back to them as I headed towards the treeline.

We fell silent again amongst the trees, the only noise was the sound of our feet crunching through the thin layer of snow on the ground.

The water in the stream was ice cold and ran clear. It certainly looked clean, at least. We filled our water bottles to the brim. I'd brought the others' water bottles too, and filled them. It felt strange, oddly sacrilegious, but we needed access to as much water as possible. We couldn't risk dehydration slowing us down. *You do whatever you have to. You get them out.* There were worse things. So I filled them and threw them in the backpack.

We made it about ten minutes past the stream when we came across the blood.

Large patches of blood-soaked snow. Bloody footprints, leading away. A trail of carnage.

Evelyn dropped to her knees next to the largest patch. She wore fingerless gloves. Her fingers curled in the snow, her bottom lip trembling, but only a tear or two slid down her cheeks. She stood abruptly, steeling herself, and without a word to either of us, she took off, following the trail of bloody footprints.

"Evelyn!" I called out to her retreating back. But she didn't turn, didn't slow. "Ev!" I didn't want to make too much noise. I turned to look at Ryan. He stood there stone faced, eying me. He didn't speak but took off after Evelyn.

I sighed deeply, pulling out the compass and checking it. It wasn't taking us too far off course, thank God. And what else could we do? We had to go.

I kept my eyes on the ground, as we walked beside the bloody trail. It was hard to tell what had happened. Too hard. I wasn't some sort of master tracker; I had limited experience identifying animal tracks and reading signs. I was decent at it, but this had been hectic. Multiple people, multiple... whatever they were. I scanned the ground and found several shells, spent cartridges, along the way. I couldn't tell how many we were following. How many had continued walking, moving this way. The prints overlapped. A group. Three or more, at least. I couldn't conclude much more than that.

The blood became fainter and fainter. The footprints turned a pale pink rather than red as we went. Eventually the blood was all but gone, but the tracks were still there to follow.

We came to a small structure, visible through the trees. A wooden shack. I didn't think it was marked on the map. Maybe an old hunter's lodge.

I put an arm out, in front of Ryan's chest, and he stopped abruptly. Evelyn came to a stop just behind us. "Shh," I said urgently, one finger over my lips. "There's a little shack or something, up ahead." I pointed through the trees. They froze, and we crouched down behind a clump of bushes. "What do we do now?" I murmured; voice pitched low. "The footprints head that way."

"What if they're inside there?" Evelyn murmured. "We need to go check."

"What if *they're* in there?" I murmured back. I didn't like the look of the latest tracks. They looked elongated, like the ones back at the hotel. I didn't like the look of them one bit, my gut was telling me not to take another step forward. To turn and run. I shook my head. "I don't like the look of the footprints. I don't think they were humans, whatever was walking this way." I swallowed thickly. "I think we should go."

Ryan hissed, a sort of chuckling whispered laugh. "You're a coward, Teddy," he said, turning and eyeing me darkly. "What if they're trapped in there? What if Katie and Dad are in there? Your Dad? Ev's? You want to just leave them? Just turn and run?" He shook his head again, and he shrugged a shoulder forward, slinging his rifle into arms reach from behind his back. "Well, I'm not; I'm going to go see what's in there."

"Look at the tracks, Ryan," I sneered back at him, cheeks flushing. "Those prints aren't human. They look just like the ones back at the hotel. If our family are in there, I hate to break it to you, but they probably aren't alive. Where do you think all that blood came from?" Evelyn let out a breath.

"Nice." Ryan chuckled again, shaking his head. He slung an arm around Evelyn's back. "It's going to be okay, Ev. I'm going in."

"Yeah?" I chuckled, "It'll be okay when we're out of here. Not a minute before. You can play the hero all you want, Ryan, but this isn't brave, it's stupid. And you could get us all killed."

Ryan just glared at me, before turning to look at Evelyn. "Stay here, okay?" he asked her. He left the baseball bat leaning against a tree and took off at a crouch towards the shack.

I stood there, frozen with indecision. I licked my lips, already dry and cracked in the cold air. "God damn it," I muttered. I turned to look at Evelyn, then back at Ryan. "Stay here, Ev." I lifted my shotgun and took off after him.

We moved slowly, weaving between trees, until we reached the treeline. The shack was in a small clearing. There was a large wood pile on the side of the little cabin. Ryan looked at me, pointed at the wood pile and then nodded at me. I nodded back in agreement. This was so stupid. I knew we'd find nothing good inside that shack, but I guess ultimately, I really couldn't stomach the thought of not looking. I didn't want to see, but part of me needed to know.

We moved quickly, still at a crouch, to the wood pile. We turned and sat with our backs to it, waiting. There was no sound, no audible movement from inside the little cabin. I realized grimly that Evelyn hadn't listened. She had followed us after all. I tried to shake my head at her, but she either didn't see me, or chose to ignore it. She moved swiftly, joining us at the woodpile, rifle in hand.

We moved around the corner a moment later, Ryan in the lead. On the other side, we found a ring of rocks, a firepit, lined with chopped logs for seats. A hide stretched off to the side, between two trees. It looked like maybe a coyote or a wolf in the middle of the tanning process. My eyes caught on a massive metal pot, like a black witch's cauldron, sitting next to the firepit.

I froze in horror and disbelief, eyes blinking rapidly, as though clearing them would somehow change what I was seeing.

The pot was filled with body parts. Mostly arms. Chopped off arms, hands flopping over the rim. A thick bloody stump, what looked like a calf, the white cross-section of bone visible. The ground nearby was covered in blood. Evelyn turned to the side and vomited into the snow. I swallowed, trying not to listen to the gagging and retching. Forcing the bile back down that was creeping up my throat. "Fuck," Ryan muttered, turning to watch her.

I moved away from them, numbly. I had to get it over with. I wanted to run. To scream. My heart pounded in my chest, and I felt like I was walking to my own gallows. A pit of horror and dread big enough to drown in opening in my stomach. Could I take it?

If I looked through that grimy, filthy window, and saw my dad? Katie? Would my mind just crack? Would I go insane?

I swallowed again, and I was already there, at the window. I stood on tiptoes and peered through the glass.

A curtain, a plaid check pattern, was half-pulled over the window, but I could still see into the cabin. It was tiny, one little room. There was a small, old-fashioned looking rough cot against one wall, a little round table and two chairs, some old dusty shelves, it was practically empty. I let out a sigh of relief. No bodies. No body parts. Nothing.

I felt my shoulders relax, sliding down from my ears, and I turned back to them, walking fully upright now. I paused for a moment, and turned and did a quick sweep, checking the other side of the little shack, just to make sure there was no one hiding behind it, waiting for us, but there was nothing there.

I made my way back over to Evelyn and Ryan. They stood in grim silence, eyes looking anywhere but at the macabre black cauldron.

"There's nothing inside. No one," I clarified. I turned away, and pulled the compass out of my pocket, before turning back to Evelyn. "You okay?" I asked her numbly.

She swallowed and nodded at me, wiping her eye with her right hand. She tucked her hair behind her ear and nodded again. "I'm fine," she managed. "Let's get the fuck out of here."

I nodded solemnly at her and focused on the compass, getting our bearings again, I pointed. "Let's head this way." We took off at a steady clip, our pace a bit faster than it had been previously. I swiveled constantly, scanning the woods around us, on the alert, shotgun at my side.

16

—·—

The next half hour or so of the hike was uneventful. I was glad in a way that I'd had the panic attack last night. I was left feeling drained, calmer, in its wake. Even still, I could feel the mounting tension. It helped that we were moving quickly, walking at a brisk pace. Not quite speed-walking, given the terrain, but enough that we were breathing heavily. That and the cold, crisp air helped to keep my head clear. Keep me focused.

Action had always been better than inaction, for me, and at least now we were moving, making progress, doing something. The waiting and the seemingly unending darkness of last night had been torture, but now the sun was out, bright and warm on our faces.

My mood lifted slightly as we walked, feeling good enough that I let my guard down. Just enough. I didn't see her until we were almost on top of her.

She stood there; the corners of her lips curved up. I would call it a smile, but there was something off, wrong about it. I didn't look like a smile so much as it looked like a reflex. A reflexive twitch, a contraction of muscles. There was no emotion behind it.

Evelyn gasped and came to a stop just behind me. I could feel her moving closer to me, pressing into my shoulder.

"Katie?" Ryan had finally noticed her too. He was standing there, staring at his little sister. She turned her gaze onto him, and the muscles in her cheeks contracted further, pulling the corners of her lips up. "What happened?" he breathed, moving closer to her.

I raised the muzzle of my shotgun, and had it trained on her forehead before anyone took another step. The click of the safety echoed in the dead air.

"What the *fuck*, Teddy." Ryan turned on me, banging the baseball bat down on the ground for emphasis, snow flying into the air. "What the fuck is your fucking problem? Huh?" I was aware of him in the periphery of my vision, but I didn't take my eyes off of Katie. I'd made that mistake last time; I wouldn't make it again. "Are you planning on shooting my entire family on sight this weekend? Like what the actual fuck?"

"That is not Katie, you fucking nitwit," I spat at him. "You saw the blood. You saw the... cabin. What the hell do you think is happening out here? You think Katie was just what... out walking around in the woods all night. Taking a little stroll? That's not her! Not anymore!" My heart was thumping now, adrenaline coursing through me. How could he possibly be this dense? Alarm bells were going off in my brain. Flashing red beacons that screamed *danger, danger*. And Katie's eyes were on mine, boring into mine, with that same cold blackness I had seen in Dr. Carter's eyes.

I flashed back to that passage in the cryptid book. About how skin-walkers could supposedly feed off your fear, use it to gain more power. How they could even jump into your body somehow. How you shouldn't ever look them in the eyes. I began to breathe heavily now, my chest heaving. I couldn't look away. Couldn't look away from those cold, dead eyes.

"Oh!" Ryan laughed, arms flinging out. "Of course it isn't. What the fuck was I thinking?"

"Ryan," Evelyn began, moving a step towards him. "Let's just calm down, okay?"

"Yeah, I don't think I will, Evelyn. How about your little boyfriend calms down, huh? How about he gives her a fucking chance to explain what happened last night. Instead of acting like a goddamn psychopath."

Evelyn turned to Katie, and my heart leapt into my throat as Katie's eyes turned on her. "Evelyn, no," I murmured, breathing as evenly as I could. "Don't go near her."

Evelyn held a hand up towards me, but she didn't take another step. She studied Katie for a moment. "Katie," Evelyn said, "what happened last night? After you left the hotel?" Evelyn swallowed audibly. "Where's my dad? Where's Dr. Ellsworth?"

They waited for her to respond, and I felt a bubble of laughter migrate up my throat. I let out a strangled laugh. "Am I losing my mind, right now? You can't be serious? You can't think that any-thing she says can possibly make a difference." I gestured towards her, taking one hand off the shotgun. "It clearly isn't her! Come on you guys!"

"Give her a chance, damn it," Ryan spat at me. "She hasn't had a chance to say a thing."

"Yeah, and since when has that ever, fucking been the case? Huh? Have you ever heard Katie not speak for this goddamn long?" I was yelling now. "Either of you?" I turned my focus on them. "She hasn't said a fucking word yet!"

I saw Evelyn's eyes widen, as she stared at me, and I knew I had convinced her. She knew I was right. She turned to look back at Katie, an expression of mingled horror and revolt on her face, and she took a stuttering step backwards. At that same moment, Katie moved forward, the muscles of her cheeks stretching her mouth impossibly wide. I raised the stock of the shotgun up against my shoulder, aiming for the center of her forehead.

Ryan came out of nowhere. He lunged, slamming into me, dropping his rifle on the ground as he went. I could sense him coming, as though he was moving in slow motion, and I watched, in horror, as Katie shot forward like a sprinter off the block. She was headed straight for Evelyn. I pulled the trigger, squeezing off a shot. I managed to pump the shotgun and squeeze the trigger again, just as Ryan's momentum carried him forward into me.

We landed on the snowy ground in a heap. He still held the baseball bat in one hand, and he slid it over my chest, using it to pin me to the ground.

I was able to lift him momentarily, angling to the right. Evelyn was screaming. But she was still standing, and Katie was nowhere in sight.

I slid a knee up under him, and shoved it into his groin, lurching upwards. Gripping the baseball bat in both hands, I used it for leverage, pushing him up and off me. I flipped him over onto the ground, as he let out an "Oof," and landed flat on his back. I let go, spinning around and scrambling for my shotgun in the snow.

Evelyn had her rifle lifted now and was pointing it off into the trees. "What happened?" I murmured, scrambling to my feet and moving towards her.

"You got her," she said, turning to me only briefly. "Hit her in the shoulder, I think. She sort of... scrambled away. She went that way, over that hill." Evelyn turned back to me, eyes wide in fear. "You were right, Teddy. It wasn't her." She was trembling slightly now, and it looked like she was going to cry. I pulled her to me with one arm, holding her against my chest.

I let her go after a minute or two, and we turned to find Ryan. Back on his feet now, hair a little mussed. He was sulking, a dark expression on his face. He eyed us wearily.

"Come on," he said, after a moment. "Let's keep going. I'm done with this shit." He brushed past us, slamming into me as he went. Evelyn and I exchanged a glance before turning to follow him.

17

— • —

I pulled Dad's compass out of my coat again. Feeling a now
familiar stab of pain every time I looked at it. I estimated we
had about another half hour or so of walking before we reached
the cars.

We had fallen silent again. I stole a glance at Evelyn, trying to
gauge how she was holding up. Her face appeared drawn and anxious. She scanned the surrounding woods constantly, eyes flickering back and forth. Something about the set of Ryan's shoulders as
he walked in front of me told me all I needed to know about how
he was feeling.

Another ten minutes or so had gone by, the forest remaining
quiet around us. The sun was growing stronger, but the wind was
picking up at the same time. I cursed it silently. Not only did it
make me feel colder, but it set branches swaying, limbs waving,
triggering my brain to think I was seeing something moving, over
and over again. I kept telling myself, it was just the wind. *Just the
wind. Just the wind.* As I marched in rhythm to the words.

But then it wasn't just the wind. We passed through a rocky
outcropping, moving through a sort of tunnel of moss-covered

boulders, and I saw it, as I came through the other side. Limbs, suddenly moving independently, in an opposing direction to the swaying trees. A trunk, and a head lifting. It peered out at me from the shadows beneath the pines, twin coal black eyes.

I raised the shotgun, heart leaping into my throat, before realizing it was just a deer. *Thank God.* I had been about to call out to the others, but I paused, shotgun lowering. The irony of finally sighting a deer this weekend and not shooting it wasn't lost on me. I sighed deeply. It started to move again, passing through the sunlight filtering through the branches overhead, striped in shadow.

It was oddly grotesque, its forelimbs far too long, its coat paler than usual, almost white. The fur on its rump and rear legs had an odd texture, an almost skin-like quality. I swallowed thickly and called out.

"There's something here." Evelyn and Ryan froze, turning back towards me. "It's a deer, but... something's wrong with it." I trained the shotgun back on the deer, aiming at its chest.

"Teddy!" Evelyn screamed. My brain was too slow to register where the danger was coming from. I scanned the length of the deformed deer's body; it froze at the sound of Evelyn's scream. I scanned the area under the trees. Were there more?

I heard a faint shifting coming from above me and to my left. I whipped around to the side, and there was Katie.

She was draped over the boulder just behind me. Scrambling over the top, she held on with both hands and one grotesquely pale foot. She had shed her coat, as well as her boots, and her hat was gone. Her pale blonde hair hung loose. Her eyes were pitch black, and her face scrunched in an awful, evil looking smile as she peered down at me.

"Hi Teddy," she crooned, grin widening as my stomach flipped sickeningly.

"No!" Ryan called out, and I could hear running footsteps behind me.

The thing that looked like Katie sprang up into an odd crouch, and I could see her pull back, muscles tense to jump.

I swung the barrel of the shotgun towards her, flicking off the safety as I went, and, moving backwards, I let off a shot just as she sprung at me.

It hit her in the chest, her body recoiling from the blast, a bloody shredded hole opening in her flesh, blooming like a rancid flower.

I took another step back, ears ringing, and pumped the shotgun, racking another shell. She landed on the ground on all fours in front of me. Her smile never faltered. I shot again, aiming for her forehead, as she lunged towards me. Fast. Too fast.

I hit her right between the eyes. Her face imploded, the blast was enough to knock her backwards, as I fell back too, stumbling over my own feet in terror.

I landed on my back, shotgun falling to the ground. I scrambled backwards on my hands and feet. Ears still ringing, I could hear screaming, faintly, in the background, like it was coming from far away. I managed to snag the strap of my shotgun and pulled it with me through the snow. I sat up and pulled it to me, aiming at Katie's slumped form. But she didn't move.

I managed to make it to my feet, and I moved away, towards the trees, on shaking legs that were suddenly too weak to carry me, seeing Katie's ruined face over and over in my mind. I looked down at my coat. I was splattered in blood. Katie's blood... or blood from whatever that... thing really was. I made it to the closest tree, stomach churning, I leaned forward, one palm against rough tree bark, and retched. My stomach spasmed over and over as it emptied onto the snowy ground.

"What the hell is happening?" Evelyn was crouched down next to Katie's body, her voice shrill. "What the actual fuck?"

I stood shakily upright, bracing myself still against the tree. I was pretty sure I was done.

We stood in silence for several minutes. Ryan eventually moved over to stand next to Evelyn. She looked up at him for a moment, then stood and put an arm around his back. He didn't react, didn't lean into her, just stood there, staring down at Katie, his face expressionless.

I watched them for a long moment, the silence eating away at me. The forest was peaceful again. Nothing but the wind blowing through the pines.

"I'm sorry, Ryan." I murmured. But it was loud enough that he could hear me. His eyes flickered up then landed on me. He stared me down for a few seconds.

"It wasn't really her." His voice was cold, hollow sounding. Then he turned abruptly and walked away.

Evelyn and I just looked at each other, faces grim. She shrugged off the backpack and pulled a water bottle out, bringing it over to me.

I rinsed my mouth, spitting into the snow. Then I forced myself to drink, my throat still raw and burning.

We moved on, after that. There was nothing more to be said. Nothing more to be done.

We pushed on at a steady, even pace. I walked with my head bowed. The encounter with Katie had left me drained, as though every ounce of energy, and drive, had been sucked from my body.

I tried to wake myself up, mentally. I patted the map, pulled out the compass, checked our position. I needed to focus. Focus on the next step. On getting us out. Before we ended up like Katie. I told myself I needed to pay better attention, be on the alert. There was no cover, nowhere we could turn our backs on safely. Just endless trees, in all directions. The next attack could come from anywhere.

And I knew there would be. Another. But if our theory was true, about them needing a... body, a host, a skin... to walk around during the day, then their numbers should be limited, at least. There was still Dr. Carter, Dr. Montgomery. My Dad.

I swallowed thickly, grief like fire sweeping through my chest at the thought of running into him next. I forced myself to take a deep breath, then another. Evelyn must have heard me, because she slowed, falling back a few steps until she was beside me.

"We should be there soon, right? The cars?" she asked, studying my face intently, a soft look in her eyes.

I nodded, through my clenched jaw. It was an effort to relax it enough to speak. "Yeah." I nodded in confirmation. "We should be coming on them any minute."

She nodded back. "We're making progress." She checked her watch. "Making good time." I shrugged a little, nodding back. "It's going to be okay, Teddy," she said gently, her voice dropping lower. I nodded at the ground, not looking at her. "You didn't have a choice, Ted," she continued, murmuring now. "You had to do it." *You do what you have to. You get them out.*

I nodded again, my inhale shaky. "Yeah. I know, Ev." I gave her the ghost of a half-hearted smile, and we continued in silence.

18

— • —

We reached the cars without any further interruptions, to find the small clearing wasn't quite just as we had left it.

I was surprised to see a third vehicle, a grey SUV, now parked on the other side of Dr. M's truck, the back covered in bumper stickers. It sat empty.

I eyed it wearily, eyes flickering back and forth between the SUV and the treeline beyond the clearing. '*Photographer on board; car makes random stops.*' I eyed a larger purple sticker just above it. '*All you need is LOVE!*' The 'O' in the shape of a peace sign. A green sticker to the right read, '*HIPPIE POWER!*' in all caps. A bright orange sticker along the bumper read, '*How am I driving?*' In bold font, and below it in smaller writing, '*How does an engine even work?* And below that, even smaller, '*How can a loving god cause such agony?*' I sighed deeply. *No kidding.*

I was a little nervous about getting into our own SUV. I figured there was a small chance Dad had left it unlocked; it's not like anyone could steal it and drive it away, not with all the tires slashed and the engine somehow disabled. But I also knew better. And knowing him, I wasn't surprised at all when I tugged on the door handle, and nothing happened.

"Fuck," Evelyn murmured behind me. "I completely forgot about the keys." She turned and let out a groan of frustration.

Ryan sighed, shoulders slumping forward, as I eyed him. I looked down at the bat in his hand. "Good thing you brought the baseball bat." He stared at me, incredulously for a moment, then down at the bat in his hand, like he'd never seen it before.

I sighed, and set my shotgun down, leaning it against a nearby tree. I walked over to him, hand held out. "Here," I said. "I'll do it." He looked at me skeptically for a second before placing the bat in my hand.

It felt oddly wrong. Strangely criminal. And I had to laugh at myself a little. I'd already done far worse than this. Would do more, if I had to. Evelyn watched me walk past her, eyes wide. I was struck again by her beauty, just then. Despite everything. She'd taken her hat off at some point. Shoved it into a pocket. I guess being shot accidentally by a hunter was fairly low on the list of concerns at the moment.

I stared at her as I marched past. Taking in the golden flecks in her green eyes, and her red curls shining like spun gold in the sun. Her hair was loose, falling around her in a mass of coils and waves, like a sort of crown. Wild and unruly. The uniqueness of every curve, the chaos of it, made my gut twist with longing. I wanted to dive my hands into it, pull her to me and hold onto her hair, while I– her expression changed, and I could tell she'd somehow read my thoughts. The gist of them, at least, as she flushed slightly, and looked away, the faintest curve to her lips.

She looked over in Ryan's direction, and I cleared my throat, forcing myself to focus. I had reached the car now. Dad's SUV. He loved this thing. Took care of it like it was his baby. I took a deep breath and felt again a wave of dissonance at the ridiculousness of feeling guilty over something so stupid, given our circumstances. I would do this and more. *You do whatever you have to do.* For her. For her, I would do whatever it took.

I knew it was true then. Deep, down in my soul. My heart. My gut. Wherever those sorts of truths reside. I would do anything. Anything I had to, today. This one day. Not only for myself, but for my dad, and for her. I had said I would burn the world for her. Lay it at her feet. Well, I guess I was getting my chance to prove it.

And I felt myself change then. Feeling oddly stronger. The energy that had left me after Katie, flooding back into me. I embraced it, leaning into it. I wouldn't be afraid. I wouldn't let the fear get to me. It would go over me, like a wave. Sift through me, like I was made of nothing but sand. Or snow, falling in the wind. And when it had gone by, there would be nothing left. Nothing left but me. And her.

I raised the bat over my shoulders, knees bent like I was waiting for a pitch. And I struck the car window as hard as I could. Over and over. The sound of the impact, of shattering glass, loud as a shot, rattling through the quiet woods.

It hadn't been as difficult as I'd expected. I used the bat to clear the area where I thought the locking mechanism would be and reached an arm carefully through; feeling around for it until my fingers fell on the rocker switch. The last thing I needed was to shred my arm on the glass. The car unlocked with a loud clunk.

It was quick enough work from there to get into the trunk and unlock the gun case. I prayed to anyone listening, thanking them that the code came easily to me.

I eyed the guns in the case. There was one more shotgun. I hesitated. Did it make sense to take it? It meant more to carry. Extra weight. We needed to move fast, and light, but what if something happened to my gun? I guessed we still had Evelyn's and Ryan's, but the thought of something happening to my shotgun still made me nervous.

There was the slick black handgun as well. Gleaming up at me. *It's not a toy, Teddy.* I pulled it from the case, its weight feeling comfortable in my hand. I would need to practice. Let off a few shots, before I felt confident with it. But I didn't really want to risk that, either. The sound would draw attention to us. It might draw them to our location.

I loaded it, checked the safety, then shoved the handgun in my belt, sliding it behind my back, and tucking my coat over it. I peered up as I did and found Ryan quickly. He was over on the far side of Dr. M's truck. Inspecting the grey SUV, peering in the windows.

There was a knife, as well. A short hunting knife. For cleaning the kill. *Skinning it,* I thought with a little fissure of irony. I took the knife, too, Ryan still peering into windows, as I slid it into my coat pocket. I grabbed extra bullets and shells, shoving my pockets full, and putting the rest into the backpack.

Evelyn didn't think there was any point in breaking into the truck. There was nothing useful she could think of, and we were wasting time, anyway. Eating up daylight.

"Let's head out, then," I called over to Ryan, on the far side of the SUV now.

Evelyn watched him for a second. "What about the SUV?" She pointed. "Its tires look fine, right?" She moved over closer. "Did you check the tires, Ryan?"

He peeked around the trunk, moving to the rear, and put a hand on the fender, crouching down. "Yeah," he called back. "I mean, they look fine to me. I don't see anything. No obvious damage."

"Why though?" I shook my head slowly. "It doesn't make any sense. Why slash our tires, disable our cars... but not this one?"

Evelyn stared at me, wide-eyed for a second, then looked back at the grey SUV, her eyes roving over the dozens of bumper stickers. "Are they targeting us, specifically, you mean?" She frowned. "It doesn't make sense." She thought for a moment. "Maybe... maybe it was all just, timing. The SUV wasn't there when we arrived, I'm sure of it. It was just us, then." I nodded in agreement. "Maybe they happened to come through here, just after we got here? Slashed the tires then."

I nodded, staring at the woods around us, scanning again. "Maybe so. That would explain it, at least."

"What a shitty coincidence, that they happened to find the cars. Maybe if we'd arrived later, our cars would have been fine, and we could have driven right out of here." She frowned in consternation, and I knew what she left unsaid. And our dads, Katie; they would still be alive.

"Maybe. Maybe it was just bad luck," I agreed. But I was struck by another thought. "Or maybe it wasn't. Maybe they didn't happen to find the cars. Maybe they were here, all along. Watching us. Maybe they watched us arrive. Waited until we left."

Evelyn's swiveled back to me, and I sensed Ryan still, watching me now too. "Katie saw one, remember? Knowing what we know now, she probably saw one, first thing that morning. She said something tall, with long arms, and legs, was following you guys, right?" I looked over at Ryan, and he watched me, a careful expression on his face. "And I thought I saw something too, just then. As we were running away from the clearing we'd camped at. I thought I saw something tall, standing in the trees, watching us."

"You did?" Evelyn frowned. I nodded, turning to her.

"Yeah, but I wasn't sure, at the time. I almost said something. But it seemed... silly. I thought it must have been my imagination. Just a tree or something, and a trick of the light." I felt a twitch of discomfort at those words. Those had been Ryan's words, at the time. And now I was just repeating them, paraphrasing. I looked back over at him.

"And your dad..." I trailed off, starting again, more slowly. "Think about what probably happened to your dad." We were all silent for a moment. "I still don't believe that was him, Ryan." I pointed back towards the way we had come from. "And now that we've seen Katie... I think it's probably safe to say the same thing happened to your dad."

Ryan shrugged, a flash of something like anger in his eyes, there one second and gone the next. "So? What's your point?" He narrowed his eyes, "You want an award or something? You want me to tell you how you were right?" He scoffed. "I just watched you shoot my sister, Teddy. I don't give a fuck what you want."

I shook my head, my cheeks flushing. "No. That's not what I'm saying, Ryan. I'm trying to say, whatever happened with your Dad, I think it must have happened quickly. Not that long after we arrived and got set up. We know they were watching us that morning. The four of us, at least. Maybe they were watching him, too. Maybe they followed him– followed all of us, from the cars." I pointed to the treeline, the edge of the clearing.

"Again, so what?" Ryan shrugged, that glint of hatred still there in his dark eyes.

"So, if they followed us from the cars..." I continued, "if they were watching us, tracking us..." I paced in a circle, eyes sweeping over the thick woods surrounding us. The wind was still blowing, gaining gusto, and I suddenly felt cold. Colder than I had been before, goosebumps rising on my arms.

I glanced up at the sky, and saw a bank of clouds had scuttered overhead, blocking the sun. The lack of warmth was immediately noticeable as the clearing dimmed. I was going somewhere with this, but we were wasting time. Time we didn't have, when we should be moving. Still, I knew I needed to follow this train of thought.

"When did they start?" Evelyn murmured quietly. I turned and looked at her, and we locked eyes. "When did they start?" She repeated louder for me. "That's what you're wondering, isn't it?" She was right. That was what my brain was trying to get at. Where it had been going. *When did it start?* At the clearing, when they happened upon our cars? Or was it earlier? Much earlier.

"The knocking," I said, and my stomach dropped. How stupid of me. The knocking, the night before. I knew the same knocking had happened back at the rental house, before we'd left for hunting the following morning. The same exact pattern, same thing that had happened at the abandoned hotel. I hadn't forgotten, but I just wasn't thinking. With everything going on, the rush to get out. To plan our route, prepare for everything that might happen, I hadn't been thinking at all about *before*. My brain wasn't running over the events before the woods, it had been too busy focusing on our current situation, to think through the chain of events that led here.

They'd been there, at the house, from the very beginning. The first night. They'd probably tracked us here from the house. They'd been following us, all along.

"They tried to lure us out, that first night, back at the house," Evelyn said, watching me as my brain ticked and whirred, hers doing the same. "They tried to get us to come out at night, with the knocking. And it worked!" She exclaimed, her eyes widening. "You did go outside, with your dad, my dad..." she trailed off. "God, Teddy. You're lucky they didn't get you then."

I felt a cold sliver of fear slice through my gut, and a trickle of dread down my spine at her words. *Fuck.* I had been staring at the ground. And I was about to look, about to raise my eyes, but I stilled, careful not to. Careful to appear like I was just listening, focusing on her words. Thinking. Careful to act normal. *Fuck, fuck, fuck.* I swallowed. *It's fine. It's all going to be fine. You're wrong. You're wrong. You're wrong.*

I raised my eyes to Evelyn's nodding slowly. I kept my voice even; a note of surprise was fine. "You're right..." I murmured, eyes locked on hers, "I guess we had no clue how close we'd come." I shook my head. "God..."

Evelyn licked her lips, nodding. She peered around the woods, eyeing the trees with suspicion. "I wonder, too..." she started and trailed off. "I wonder about them, you know, the old couple. Mr. and Mrs. Johnson, wasn't it?" She looked back at me, eyebrows raised. "There was something... off about them. Didn't you think so?"

I thought for a moment, eyes widening, remembering how I hadn't wanted to touch the cookies. The book. I'd read the whole chapter about the people who went missing, up in these woods. They had mentioned the older woman who disappeared, how she wore a red coat, but not the boy. They never mentioned that about the boy, and the book was very detailed.

I nodded slowly, looking over at her. "Yeah, Ev. I did. There was something strange about them." I nodded. "I remember feeling that, too." She nodded back at me, a somewhat triumphant look on her face. It wasn't much. This small victory. It did nothing to help us escape. Nothing to get us out of here. But it was information. Clues. It was something. We knew more now, had figured out more now, than we had earlier.

Ryan let out a scoffing laugh. "The old couple?" He shook his head in disbelief, looking back and forth between us. Like we were crazy. "You've got to be kidding me." He shrugged, arms lifted out to his sides, his rifle swaying behind his back with the motion. "Who's next? Huh?" He laughed again, an incredulous expression on his face. "You know, Ev, your mom was acting a little funny, that night, right? Or hey... you know, now that I think about it, there was this guy, at the gas station, back in Burlington. He was sort of suspicious, too. Maybe he followed us from there, you know?" He paused, eyes flickering back and forth between us. "Are you both insane?"

Evelyn sighed, rolling her eyes and turning away from him. She turned her back to us, facing the treeline and walked away a few paces. "God, Ryan. Do you always have to be such a buzzkill?" she muttered.

"Hey, here's an idea," he continued without pausing to respond. "How about, we take the fucking bat, and we break into the SUV?" He pointed back at the grey vehicle. "I mean, the tires aren't slashed, right? Odds are they haven't messed with it. Since, you know, we're the ones they've been tracking for weeks, or whatever." He smirked over at me. "Why don't we focus on getting the fuck out of here, not on playing amateur detectives? Hmm?"

He walked over towards me, and I stiffened involuntarily. "Give me the bat, Teddy." He held his hand out to me. I lifted it reluctantly, and he grasped onto the swinging end, pulling it out of my hand and eyeing me with a look of general disgust.

He leaned in close to me, and I managed not to flinch. His voice dropped to a whisper. "You think you're such a fucking hero, don't you? *Boy scout*," he spat at me, his voice pitched low. "Well, guess what? I'm going to be the one to get us out. Watch me drive us the fuck out of here."

I breathed in deeply and nodded, eyes never leaving his. "Be my guest, Ryan." I gestured towards the SUV. "That would be great."

He just threw me one last glare and moved over to the SUV. He shrugged his rifle off as he went. Propping it up against the rear bumper. He moved around to the other side of the SUV, to the passenger window.

I stood there, frozen with indecision, eyeing the rifle. I was across the clearing still, past my dad's SUV. He was much closer, but the cars partially blocked his view of me. I'd never seen him set the rifle down. Not once.

I began to move closer, walking slowly, casually. He swung, and I caught a flash of movement, but the sound, the glass shattering, tinkling down, still made me jump slightly. I couldn't hear the lock click from here, but he must have found the switch quickly; he was moving back around the rear of the SUV before I knew it, scooping up the rifle and slinging it back over his shoulder. He moved over to the driver's side, climbing in.

"Do you know how to hotwire a car? Or what?" Evelyn called out to him; arms crossed over her chest. He eyed her sideways and continued to fiddle around in the car. I watched as he reached to open the glove compartment, then slid a hand up, underneath the sun visor. He was searching for a key.

And apparently, he didn't find one. He slammed his hands into the steering wheel in frustration, accidentally hitting the car horn. The blast shattered the silence, shocking me momentarily. "Fuck!" he screamed.

"So... that's a no, then," Evelyn said sarcastically. "Great." She turned and leaned against the side of her dad's truck. "Looks like we're still trapped here."

I shrugged, shaking my head. I cleared my throat after a moment. It wasn't the worst idea. It was unlikely they'd locked the keys inside, obviously. But maybe a spare key... you never knew. It was worth trying. I felt a fissure of doubt, mixing with the nagging feeling of dread in the back of my mind, causing a dissonance I really didn't care for.

"We really should get going," I called out to them, eying the surrounding woods. I shrugged my sleeve down, peering at my watch. We'd wasted too much time already, and who knows how far the sound of that horn had traveled. And who, or what, had heard it.

I pulled the map out of my pocket quickly. I wanted to get my bearings again, now that we'd taken the detour to the cars, confirm our heading. I moved over to my Dad's SUV, spreading the map out on the hood, pulling his compass out of my pocket. I was standing right where we stood together, just yesterday morning. I looked down at the map and my vision blurred slightly. I wiped my eyes hastily, hoping Evelyn hadn't seen. There was no time. No room for that, and no time.

I eyed the map, and our location at the cars. We had traveled slightly south, but we were still just essentially west of Mount Snow. Our path would take us through a more heavily visited area of the National Forest. There was the trail there; we stood a decent chance of running into other hunters, or hikers even, near or on that trail. There was still the hope of running into someone who could help us. Someone with a working vehicle.

I held up the compass, and eyed the sun above, barely visible through the now thick and heavy cloud cover. *Damn it.* We didn't need more snow. Maybe an inch, inch and a half had fallen last night. Not enough to slow us down, but more significant snowfall would. It wasn't the end of the world, but it certainly didn't work in our favor.

Besides, I thought, with a punch to the gut, snow meant tracks. The snow cover so far had been fairly spotty, under the thick trees; it wasn't consistent. That made it harder to track. But with more fresh snow, a thick cover, we would leave a clearer trail of footprints behind us. A blaring signal for anyone to follow.

Fuck. I cursed myself again. I liked to think of myself as smart, but I hadn't thought of that. It hadn't occurred to me to worry about them tracking us by our own footprints. That's what I would do, if I were them. That's what a hunter would do. And I had no doubt in my mind that was what they were.

188

"No!" Evelyn cried out. A moaning, keening sort of cry. And my blood ran hot, like fire ripping through my veins. I whirled around, shotgun already in my hands somehow, and I searched the vicinity of the cars.

Ryan stood there, off to the left. He'd climbed out of the grey SUV and was staring across the clearing. I turned swiftly. Evelyn was there in the middle of the clearing. She'd fallen to her knees. "No, no, no," she was sobbing, breathlessly, but her hands were moving, searching for her rifle, slung over her shoulders.

I swung the barrel up and to the right, in the direction she was looking, but I already knew what I would find.

Dr. Montgomery stood there, just on the edge of the clearing. He turned to me, eyes locking onto mine. They were dark, but then again, they always had been. I didn't see the same coldness to them that I had with Dr. C. He eyed my shotgun, raising both hands in a gesture of surrender. "It's okay, Evelyn," he murmured, his voice soothing. "Everything's fine. It's me. I promise."

Evelyn sobbed harder, leaning forward, her voice wracked with pain. I moved closer to her, closing the distance across the clearing, and Dr. M paused, mid-step. He nodded to me. "It's okay, Teddy. I'm not a threat." He met my eyes. "Do you hear me? I am not a threat to you." He shook his head, looking back and forth between us. "I'm so glad I found you kids. You have no idea..." he trailed off. "We got separated last night. I've been walking. For ages."

"No." Evelyn shook her head. "No!" Then she fell silent. I thought she'd stopped crying for a moment. But her shoulders shook. Silent tears, no sound coming out as she struggled for each breath.

"I got turned around; had no clue where I was. I've been wandering in circles, probably." He shrugged, grinning at me in a self-deprecating sort of way, and my stomach clenched, gut twisting. I felt tears springing to my eyes. He was so like him. So real. It was exactly the sort of way he would smile. I couldn't... I couldn't.

Evelyn looked up at me, her cheeks streaked with the tracks tears had left behind, her nose flushed red. "Teddy..." She shook her head at me, and her face crumpled as she started to cry again. I had tears running down my cheeks now, too, I knew. Just a few. I blinked rapidly, trying to control them. *Breathe.* I told myself. *Breathe.* I forced my body to still, to calm. *Focus.* Deep, even breaths. It was working, I stilled, raising the shotgun higher, I aimed at his chest this time. Fell into that familiar stance. I flicked the safety off by feel, not needing to look.

Evelyn's face twisted again, and she looked away from me, back at her dad. "How?" she managed, between sobs. "How did you survive the night? Out here, all alone? How?" She bent forward again, gripping her midsection, arms hugging, squeezing, like she was holding herself together. "How is that possible?"

I could hear it. The note of hope in her voice. She wanted to believe it. Wanted to believe it was really him. That it was possible he had survived somehow. Had been out wandering alone under the trees for hours. But at the same time, she knew, had to know, that the odds of that were extremely slim.

But he was so like himself. So realistic and convincing, that I wasn't sure. Even I couldn't be sure. Not yet. My mind raced and my heart started to pound again in my chest. How could we tell? How? No. I had to stay calm. Had to breathe. Stay calm. There would be a way. There had to be a way. I would know.

But I was starting to feel panicky now. Wracked with uncertainty. My gut seemed to be abandoning me, right when I needed it.

"What's my middle name?" Evelyn asked, pausing in her sobbing.

"What?" Dr. Montgomery sputtered, scoffing slightly.

"I said, what's my middle name?" Evelyn struggled to take a deep breath, a strangled sob escaping. She pressed her hands down on the ground and pushed herself unsteadily to her feet.

"Teddy," Ryan called out from behind us. "Put the gun down. There's no reason not to listen to him. Hear him out. Come on..."

"What's my middle name? Huh?" She waited a beat, but he didn't answer. "How about my birthday?" she continued, "When is my birthday?" Nothing. Eyes darting. She sobbed harder, "What do you make for Christmas dinner every year? What's Mom's favorite food?" Evelyn was on her feet now, trembling, practically screaming the questions at him, her voice wracked with despair. He scoffed again.

"Evelyn, honey, just calm down." He raised his hands again. But I could tell he looked nervous now. His eyes narrowed slightly.

I felt a pit of dread open up in my stomach. *It's not him. It's not him.* Evelyn turned away from him then, sobbing, and she looked at me, and shook her head. The briefest of movements. But it was enough. I raised the muzzle of the shotgun and centered on his chest. Where his heart would be.

A howl went up, bone chilling, splintering the silence of the clearing. Dr. M's face changed, distorting into a rabid-looking growl, and I pulled the trigger as he darted forward.

I hit him square in the chest. Pumping the shotgun, I took aim again, meaning to go for his head, I hit him in the neck as he moved past me in a blur. He was going for Evelyn, and the first shot hadn't taken him down, but a cloud of red mist floated in the air as I hit him in the neck. Turning and moving swiftly behind him, I pumped again and hit the back of his head. His head pitched forward as a black hole appeared.

The howling was moving closer now. I turned to the side, as he fell to the ground. Evelyn was running now, back towards the cars. A flash of movement to my left.

I swung the shotgun up as a ball of pale fur exploded from low in the tree line. A wolf. A coyote. Something. Coal black eyes and snarling fangs. Slobber dripping from its maw. I blasted it in the face. Letting off two shots, pumping the shotgun in between with a satisfying *thunk*. My ears were ringing, my head buzzing.

I didn't stop. Didn't pause as the wolf hit the ground and slid several feet in the snow. It hit me in the legs and took me down momentarily. I scrambled backwards, managing to hold onto the shotgun.

I rose to my feet, slipping slightly in the snow, and ran towards the cars. Evelyn was behind the SUV, rifle raised in her hands, aiming towards me, and the wolf that lay still on the ground. Another howl went up, off further in the distance this time. "Let's go!" I called out to them. Ryan moved out from between the truck and grey SUV, rifle in hand.

"Let's get the fuck out of here!" he called back. We turned together and ran. I pointed off to the left as we went.

"This way," I murmured breathlessly. Then a moment later. "Fuck!" I patted my pocket. "Wait, the map! I left the fucking map." I groaned and started to turn back. "You guys keep going, head in this direction, I'll grab it." How mind-numbingly stupid of me.

"Teddy!" Evelyn called out. She pulled something out of her pocket, holding it aloft for me to see. "I got it," she called back, "come on!" Her cheeks were still streaked with tears. I nodded. We turned, and we ran.

19

— · —

The howling trailed off in the distance, and I could tell after a while that they were falling behind rather than gaining on us.

We slowed our pace, eventually. It wasn't possible to maintain running like that for long. I wondered if the same thing was true for them. They seemed to move quickly in short bursts, over short distances, but maybe they didn't have great endurance. Maybe they couldn't maintain that speed for long.

I reloaded my shotgun as we went. I felt myself falling deeper into despair as we continued to walk, feeling more and more demoralized. Once again, now that the adrenaline was starting to wear off a bit, I was beginning to feel anxious. I tried to focus on a rhythm as we walked.

But overall, I was less worried about myself than I was about Evelyn. She continued to cry randomly. She would be fine for a while, and then I would look over to find silent tears rolling down her cheeks again. She brushed them away, refusing to look at me.

I felt like I should say something. Try to comfort her. But I'd always been terrible at that. I never knew what to say when someone died. Other than sorry. *Sorry for your loss?* So contrite, conveying none of the feeling behind it, the emotion... not possible to put into words. If there was anything I hated, it was being fake. And if I couldn't say anything real, I'd rather not say anything at all.

I'd been terrible, horrible at offering condolences, standing uselessly by the wall at every funeral I'd been to. And this felt no different.

I told myself she didn't want to talk about it yet, anyway. At least that's what I took the lack of eye contact to mean. So, we walked together in silence, aside from the occasional sniffle. I watched Evelyn, and Ryan, keeping my mind occupied between keeping one eye on them, and one on the surrounding woods.

An hour went by. Then two. We were moving out of the Glastenbury Wilderness, and into the less heavily forested area on the map. The lack of cover made me nervous.

It was easier to see someone coming, but it also left me feeling like we were oddly exposed. I picked up the pace, pushing faster. "I think it's only about two miles, through here, until we get back into the woods again," I spoke up, breaking the silence. "I think we should push faster here. I don't like being out in the open like this." Evelyn nodded grimly, picking up the pace. Ryan sighed loudly but nodded his agreement. I continued to look back behind us, watching for anyone trailing us. But if they were there, they somehow managed to stay hidden.

Once back under the cover of the forest, we stopped for a few minutes to rest. I brought out the protein bars and passed them around.

Evelyn just shook her head, mouth drawn in a grim line. "Come on, Ev, you need to eat something."

"I can't Teddy." She shook her head again. "I just can't right now."

I sighed, sitting down heavily beside her. "I get it," I said, "But you're burning a lot of calories, and we've got miles left to go. You need to keep your strength up."

She nodded grimly. "I know. I'll try again in a little bit, okay?"

I nodded, letting it go. Ryan and I ate quickly, downing the protein bars with water. We all took a quick bathroom break. Standing guard while the others went off behind some trees. I went as fast as I could, anxious the whole time.

Ryan and Evelyn were still standing there, just where I had left them, when I got back. I breathed a sigh of relief, and we continued on our way.

I made sure to check our heading with the compass, at least every fifteen minutes or so. I knew how easy it was to veer off course. A light snow began to fall eventually, the heavy grey clouds overhead that had been threatening us all day, finally letting loose.

I watched the snowflakes falling around us, in large white puffs, and the woods felt strangely peaceful again, at that moment. I had come to see it as a menacing, dangerous place, and as true as that was, it was also beautiful, too.

I was finally feeling a little more at ease. We had to be more than halfway there by now, and I was starting to feel more hopeful that this might actually work, that we would really make it out. I was just thinking about what our next move should be; if we reached Mount Snow and no one was there, should we walk straight to the house? I was lost in my thoughts when a woman walked out from behind a clump of trees.

I heard Evelyn gasp, just as I spotted her, and we came to a halt. She was wearing hiking gear, a backpack, with the strap clipped around her waist. A man stepped out of the woods behind her.

We stood there, staring at them. The woman looked at the man, frowning, "Hi?" she said, but it came out more like a question.

"H-hi," Evelyn murmured, taking a step forward. "You're here, hiking?" she asked, eagerly.

"Yes..." The man said, moving closer, and standing half in front of the woman, eyes on the shotgun I must have grabbed instinctually. I saw his gaze drift up to my coat. To the splatters of blood.

"Where..." Evelyn trailed off. "How did you get here? Do you have a car?" Her bottom lip trembled slightly.

"Ev–" I started, but she cut me off, continuing.

"I'm sorry, I'm sure I sound like a crazy person. My dad..." she trailed off, "we were here, hunting with a larger group. We–we've been attacked. We need help. We've been walking for hours. Our cars, the tires were slashed. We're trying to walk to Mount Snow." She was starting to ramble now.

The woman's eyes widened. "Attacked? Attacked by who?" She frowned over at me, then at Ryan, a suspicious glint in her eyes.

"We ran away from them," Evelyn said. "But we need to get out of here, fast. Do you have a car? A way to drive out? Please," she added. "Please, it's not safe here. We really need your help."

They looked at each other for a long moment. And the man stepped forward, both hands up. "Listen, we want to help you... but those guns." He pointed back and forth between us, "Are making us a little nervous." His gaze landed on me. "And why are you covered in blood?"

I shook my head, letting go of the shotgun. It swung back and forth at my side. "Look, I can only imagine how this looks, but she's telling the truth. We were attacked. We spent last night camping out in the abandoned town up in the Glastenbury Wilderness. The rest of our family disappeared during the night." I opened my mouth, and the words tumbled out. The story was plausible enough, for having no real plan formulated yet for what we were going to say. I hadn't gotten around to worrying about just how on earth we were going to explain what had happened up here in these woods. This wasn't the worst explanation, as long as we glossed over the details.

"My dad," I continued. "Her dad," I pointed at Evelyn, then over at Ryan. "His dad, and sister..." I shook my head. "They're all gone. We've been navigating by compass, and a map. Trying to walk our way out. Please." I kept my hands raised, away from my gun. "These guns were for hunting. We don't mean anyone any harm. Please, you have to believe us."

The man turned halfway towards the woman, still keeping an eye on us. I could see them deliberating, having their own little conversation just with their eyes.

He came out of nowhere from behind them. Dr. Carter grabbed the man's head, hands on either side, and twisted. I heard his neck snap with a sickening crunch.

I began to reach for my shotgun, fumbling. The woman was screaming bloody murder. I couldn't hear anything else. Katie came at us from the left. I never heard her footsteps on the frozen ground. I caught a flash of movement in my periphery, and when I turned, and saw it was her, I froze, in terror. It was only a split second, but it was enough; she was on me.

I landed heavily on my back, the air rushing from my chest as she landed on top of me. She crouched there; mouth split in a wicked smile. Dried blood coating her hair, her face, the front of her shirt. A dark red stain in the center of her chest. I could see a hole in the middle of her shirt, from where I had shot her.

I had landed on the handgun, and my back screamed in agony. She shoved me down as I tried to rise, both hands pressing on my chest. "Don't worry, Teddy," she crooned at me. "I'll make it quick. Just like you did for me." My heart was in my throat, panic buzzing through my body, making me slow. Stupid. My shotgun lay off to the side, to my right, just a few feet away. It may as well have been miles.

The knife, I remembered. If I could just get my hand into my coat pocket. But she was straddling me, pinning me to the ground. I struggled against her. A shot rang out from my right. Then another. Katie was hit, the momentum knocking her off balance long enough, allowing me to get the upper hand. I pushed her off me, raising up, one hand snaking behind my back. She was hit, but she wasn't down. She reeled back at me, blood spraying from her neck out into the snow. I fumbled for a second with the safety on the unfamiliar gun.

I clicked it off, raising it to her forehead. I shot her right between the eyes. Her head lolling backwards, body following it. I pushed her off me, sliding my legs out from under her, scrambling to my feet. I went for my shotgun first.

I turned to find Dr. Montgomery, his face feet away from mine, as he lunged at me. I raised the handgun and aimed. Two quick shots to the head, and he was down. Falling into the snow. Twitching for a moment, then still.

I reached the shotgun, grabbing it, heart pounding, I turned to look for Evelyn. She was standing there with the rifle aimed at her dad. A horrified expression on her face. It struck me as almost comical, in that moment. And I knew it wasn't funny, that I was just in shock, but I almost started laughing. I shook my head to clear it. She was okay. Thank God, she was okay.

I looked for Ryan. He had his rifle raised as well. He was shooting at his dad. I watched as snow kicked up off the ground. Dr. Carter was moving steadily closer to us, but he stopped and turned towards Ryan as he backed away.

He must have taken out the woman first. Her lifeless body lay on the ground beside the man's. Probably her husband. I was filled with rage, suddenly at the thought. This poor couple had been hiking in the woods, having a normal day, and we had shown up out of nowhere, and ruined their lives. Now they were both dead. For no reason. Just for having been in the wrong place, at the wrong time.

A scream ripped out of my throat. I leveled the handgun again and fired at his back. Hitting him again and again, until I was out of bullets, emptying the clip. I raised the shotgun next, dropping the handgun on the snow.

I walked up to his body, where it lay on the ground. And I shot him point blank in the back of the head.

I looked up at Ryan first. He said nothing. Slowly lowering the rifle, his chest heaving, rising and falling as he breathed heavily. Our eyes met and he just shook his head at me. This was unreal. This couldn't be real.

I turned, scanning the woods around us, shotgun still raised. "They come back?" Evelyn's voice was incredulous, crying again, tears streaming down her face. She looked down at Katie's body. Her Dad's. "They come back?" She shook her head. She was in shock, too, I thought numbly.

I turned, spun around in one spot, eyeing the tree line around us. I could see the trail now, the one the couple must have been following, off to our right, up ahead. We'd reached the trail. Only a few miles left to go now. We were close. We were so close.

I staggered, staring at the cold, lifeless trees as they blew in the wind. The snow falling on the bodies that littered the ground. "Where are you?" I screamed. "Where are you? Huh? Come out! I'm ready for you! I'm waiting..." I trailed off, my voice cracking. "Come out!" I fell to my knees, dropping the shotgun, and sobbed into my hands.

I didn't care anymore. Didn't care that Ryan was watching me blabber like a baby. That Evelyn saw. I didn't care.

He had to be out there, somewhere. Why hadn't we seen him yet? They'd come for us twice now, but him... nothing. Where was he? Was he out there, watching us right now? Hiding in the shadows? What was he waiting for? I sobbed until my chest hurt. Until I was too congested to breathe. I felt Evleyn come sit with me, at some point, arms wrapped around my shoulders. She held me, while I shook with tears.

I stopped, eventually, and when I stood, Ryan was standing off in the distance, his back to us. He turned to look at me, and I expected him to be sneering. But he didn't sneer. Didn't laugh. He only stared at me for a long moment, a sadness in his eyes, before turning away again.

Evelyn cupped my face in her hands. "It's going to be okay Teddy. This is all going to be over soon." I nodded, half listening. "We have to keep going. We're going to get out of here. We're going to walk out on our own. Nothing is going to stop us. Okay? Nothing." I nodded again. I retrieved the handgun, reloading it. And we moved on. Somehow. We moved on. And we kept walking. Just us, and the falling snow.

20

— • —

I hated to stop. The sun, no longer overhead, was making its downward arc now. Our hours of daylight were numbered. I had thought of one last possibility. One last shortcut.

I wanted to check the map again, and besides, there was probably no better time than now. We'd just brought them down, again. With any luck, it took a few hours for them to... regenerate, or whatever the fuck it was they did. Now might be our best chance to escape.

Evelyn got out the map, helping me to hold it upright, as I scanned the area near trail #326. I located it quickly. Something my brain had taken in but hadn't really registered. The little icon of a hut, just to the right of the trail. It wouldn't take us out of our way. I had no clue what it was, but I was hoping maybe it was some sort of Ranger station. Maybe there would be someone there who could help us. If not, maybe we would find a phone.

I explained my plan quickly, and Evelyn's face lit up a little as she listened. It was worth a shot, we decided. Ryan only shrugged in agreement. He had seemed somewhat despondent, since the hikers. Keeping quiet and keeping to himself.

I made sure Evelyn walked beside me as we headed for the hut. I picked up the pace a little as we got closer. I could see it up ahead, through the trees. I looped my arm into hers, forcing her to move faster. She looked up at me, head darting up in surprise, a slight frown on her face. But I just shook my head no, imperceptibly, and we kept going.

We reached the little ranger's station, the size of a large closet, with Ryan close to fifty yards behind us. I tried the handle first, but no such luck. I peered through the little window, but I could see the lights were off. There was no one there. I lifted my shotgun, turning it so the stock of the gun faced forward. "Stand back," I said to Evelyn, and I slammed the gun forward, into the glass. It shattered instantly.

I reached my arm through, clearing broken shards of glass as I went with the sleeve of my coat, and at this angle, I could just reach the handle from the inside.

I unlocked the door, pushing it in, and I turned and grabbed Evelyn's hand, pulling her inside with me, and shutting the door behind us. I moved to the back of the small cabin. There was a desk there, with a red phone sitting on it. I ran over and lifted the phone to my ear, holding it back over my hearing aid where the mics were. I listened for a dial tone, heart pounding. But there was only silence. "God damn it." I turned and handed it out to Evelyn. She held it to her ear for a minute, then shook her head at me.

I turned, and put my back against the far wall, eying the door. There were no other windows to worry about. "Teddy?" She frowned over at me, as I slid to the ground, back sliding down the wall, and sat for a moment, resting my head against the wall, eyes on the ceiling.

"Is something wrong?" she asked.

I just sighed deeply, trying to formulate my words. What I needed to say next.

"Are you having a panic attack?" she asked. I shook my head, reaching forward to grab her hand, I pulled her gently down, until she sat next to me.

"No, Ev." I shook my head again. "I'm not. Listen..." I didn't know how to begin. "It's... it's Ryan, okay?"

Her frown deepened, brows crinkling in confusion. "Ryan? What about Ryan?"

"I wanted to get us here, come inside ahead of him." I nodded towards the door. To where he must be lingering now. "Because... because I don't think he can come inside, Ev."

I watched her for a moment, studying her face for a reaction. But she just stared at me, brows wrinkled. "But I'm not sure," I continued. "And I... I wanted to be sure." It took her a long, aching moment to get what I meant. I saw the confusion transition to understanding in her eyes.

"No." She shook her head. "Teddy." She lay a hand on my arm. "No, that– that can't be. Teddy," she continued gently, "you're wrong, this time." I started to shake my head, but she continued, "I know how... how crazy this has been, and we're all on edge. But you're just scared. You're freaked out. You can't possibly be right."

"I think I am, Ev." I shook my head. "I don't want to be, but–"

"But he never left us." She shook her head. "He's been with us the whole time, remember? Even at night, right?" She nodded encouragingly at me. "I know I fell asleep for a bit, at the old hotel. But you, you stayed awake. You watched over us. You know he didn't leave, right? He was there the whole time. He was sleeping right next to me; I woke up and he was right there." She shook her head again and pointed at the door. "That's really him, Teddy, I swear. You don't need to worry."

"I know, Ev. I know he never left that night. But that's not when it happened."

She frowned at me. She looked a little frightened now, almost. Of me. I realized. She thought I was losing it. I continued, "It was the first night. At the house. I didn't realize it until we talked the timeline through, at the cars, but you were right. They were there, outside the house, that first night, trying to lure us out. And remember, he went outside that night. He walked back. Alone. He left the house late and walked back to their rental." I felt my eyes sting and blinked them rapidly. "That had to have been when... when they got him."

She was shaking her head still, in disbelief. But I could see the doubt in her eyes. She licked her lips. "Teddy, why would you even think of that? It doesn't make any sense. You think the real Ryan is... dead? That he's been one of them, this entire time? And he just... what? Got ready the next morning, and piled in the car to go hunting with us? This is nuts, Teddy. It's..." She looked at me with real fear now and sat back slightly. "It's crazy, Teddy. It's not possible."

"I'm telling you; it is possible Ev. I know it sounds crazy, but something has been off with him. Since that morning. He was acting weird at breakfast, he came and offered me coffee, he–"

She pulled back further and got to her feet. "Coffee, Teddy? That's what made you suspicious? He offered you coffee." She put her hands on her hips, tilting her head at me.

"No... it's... when he offered me coffee, he asked me if something was wrong. It was like he didn't even remember what had happened the night before. Didn't know that I'd overheard you two."

"Okay..." Evelyn frowned, "maybe he forgot for a second. You know how he is; he's not the most sensitive person." She thought for a moment. I got to my feet, peering across the room at the window. "Besides, he did remember. He said something about it later, when you first suspected Dr. Carter. He said something to me, like 'See, I told you so,' when you first pulled the gun on him."

I was already shaking my head before she could finish. "No. I get it seemed that way. But he knew because I told him." She stared at me in confusion. "When he asked me why I was upset that morning, I reminded him of what had happened. I even repeated part of what he had said. About me bringing a gun to school... being a psychopath. I thought he was just messing with me, but now I realize he didn't have any clue what I was talking about. I thought he was acting a little odd, at the time. But I had no idea what it meant."

"No, Teddy." She was shaking her head, but her face fell. Her lips trembling a little. "No, it still doesn't make any sense. Why would he do this? If he's one of them…" Her eyes were damp with tears now, as she pointed at the door. "Why on earth would he do all this? Stay with us overnight. All day today. Walk with us, pretend like he's one of us? Why?"

"I don't know, Ev–" I started, taking a step towards her, but she cut me off again, holding up a hand.

"No. It's not possible. He fought against them, fought with us."

"Did he?" I asked, eyebrows raised. "Did he, Ev? I think he shot, what? Once, maybe twice, and only this last time that they attacked us. And his bullets were hitting the ground at his dad's feet. He never actually shot him. He never stepped in to help or save either of us." I shrugged. "He didn't stop us, but he didn't really help us either." I thought for a moment. "Actually, I take that back. With Katie, he did try to stop me. He knocked me to the ground, remember?"

"Because he thought she was his sister, Teddy." She was yelling now, gesturing wildly, her voice exasperated. "That doesn't prove anything. It would make no sense, none at all, for him to just– go along with everything, this whole time. Why didn't he help *them* then? Turn and attack us when they did, if he's one of them. This is crazy, Teddy, can't you see that?"

I nodded slowly, eyes on the ground now, hair falling over my face. "Okay," I said slowly. I paused for a moment, hiding from her eyes on me. I understood it. I really did. But it still stung. The uncertainty, and the fear I saw there. "Okay," I said, "I get it. I know how I sound. I realize I sound crazy."

I looked up at her, and saw she was calmer now, staring at me, her green eyes no longer frightened. Just... sad. "Remember, I said I wasn't sure." I swallowed. "But there have been other things... other things that I... that made me think something wasn't right with him. But you're right, it is crazy. And I can't be sure." I shook my head. "But if I'm wrong, Evelyn... and trust me, I hope I am... but if I am wrong, then where is he?"

I lifted my arm and pointed at the door. At the broken glass. "Where is he, right now?" I stood there, waiting, eyes stinging again. She appeared frozen, eyes wide, staring back at me. "Why isn't he in here? Why isn't he walking through the door? Why is he still out there, just... just waiting?"

She shook her head slowly, glancing over at the door. She turned away from me, arms crossed over her chest. I moved over to her, took hold of her arms, turning her gently to face me. She looked away and wouldn't meet my eyes.

"Listen, please, Ev. He was able to come inside at the old hotel, but my dad invited us in, technically. He said something like, 'Come on in boys.'" She scoffed, shaking her head. "And something similar happened earlier, at the rental house. I think he was lingering outside, on the porch, wasn't moving through the door, until his dad told him to come in." She snorted again, but her face crumpled in a bit, one tear sliding down her cheek. "I knew in my gut something was wrong, but until you said what you did... I just... it never occurred to me that they could have got to him that first night. In my mind, that was before everything started."

She was crying now, silently, tears streaming down her cheeks, I pulled her close to me, held her against my chest. "I'm sorry, Ev. I'm so– I'm so sorry. And I was hoping that I was wrong. I didn't want to confront him. Didn't want to believe it... I guess I thought if we could find another house, another place he hadn't been in before, then maybe I could test it. Bring him here and see if he would come inside, on his own. But he's not, Ev. He's not."

She was sobbing harder now, holding on to the collar of my coat. She pulled back from me, wiping at her eyes with both hands. "Please, believe me, Ev, I'm not– I'm not crazy, I'm not some–"

"I know that, Teddy. I know." She peered up at me, her green eyes wet with tears. "I trust you. I do. This is all just... it's all just too much. I can't–" She stopped, shaking her head, staring off towards the door, then back at me. She reached up, and cupped my face in her hands, eyes flickering back and forth, studying my features. "I love you, Teddy," she said quietly. "You know that, right?"

I shook my head, half laughing, half sobbing. "You do?"

"Yeah," she said, nodding, smiling now through the tears streaming down her face. "Yeah, I do."

I grinned back at her. "I love you too, Ev," I whispered. I leaned in and kissed her. Kissed her like I was dying. Like she was, too. Like I would never get to kiss her again. Because for all I knew, I wouldn't.

She let me go, eventually. We'd wasted too much time already. It had been about fifteen minutes or so, I guessed. Fifteen minutes, and he hadn't come through the door. Hadn't even tried.

She held onto my hand until the last possible second, my fingertips sliding through hers. I turned back at the door, to check. She was standing there, rifle gripped tightly in both hands. She nodded that she was ready.

21

— • —

I pushed the door open and stepped out onto the little porch, worn wooden boards creaking underneath my feet.

He was there, about twenty yards away. He stood behind a tree. Half of his body, and his face, hidden. He held the baseball bat down at his side, waiting for me.

I lifted my shotgun and trained it on him. I could hit him in the shoulder from here, or in the side of his gut, but it wouldn't do much damage. Wouldn't be enough to take him down, as temporary as that would be.

I stilled, and stayed that way for a minute or so, thinking. What was my next move? Why wasn't he aiming back, ready with his rifle? I felt a little bubble of panic growing, as I scanned the silent forest surrounding us. There was no one visible lurking under the trees, but that didn't mean they weren't there.

Were there others? Other hunters, like us, or hikers, that they'd stolen the forms of? Were they waiting out there, ready to ambush us? Was there something I was missing?

But my panicked thoughts amounted to nothing, and I knew I was wasting time. Wasting daylight. I stepped down off the porch and called out to him.

"What is this? Hide and seek?" I waited for his response, but none came. I continued. "I can see you, you know. You never were very good at hiding…" I trailed off, muttering the last part more to myself, my mind flickering back to us, as kids. Playing hide and seek. Ghost in the graveyard. I saw him as he was, back then, in my mind's eye. But if I was right, that wasn't him. I couldn't let him scare me. Let fear get the best of me. We were both armed, but I was a better shot, if it came down to that. I had the advantage.

I moved a few steps closer, feet crunching on snow, revealing pine needles and leaves in my wake. I lifted the shotgun higher, sighting him in, and I began to walk forward but angled to the left, as well.

"Why, Ryan?" I called out. "Or whatever your name is." Still nothing but silence. The bat gripped loosely in his hand, his stance one of readiness, oddly threatening. "Why pretend? Why stay with us all day? Why didn't you fight with them? Why haven't you tried to stop us? Kill us when you had the chance?" Nothing but the wind. "What were you going to do, let us walk out of here?" I chuckled a little. "What was your plan?"

He laughed then, a low chuckle that sent a shiver down my spine. I continued my slow, steady march around the tree, trying to get to a better angle. "You still don't get it, do you?"

"No, I guess I don't," I said evenly. "Why don't you explain it to me." The back of his head was just visible behind the tree.

213

"Teddy! Left!" Evelyn's voice rang out, and I spun to my left, just as the crack of her rifle rebounded, echoing through the forest.

A streak of white, moving low. I took aim quickly and shot. The coyote fumbled, almost tripping over its own feet. But it managed to recover, and it kept coming. I aimed at the crown of its head and fired again. This time the shot hit home.

My ears were still ringing, sounds around me muffled, but I felt a woosh of air next to my head, and I could faintly make out Evelyn's voice in the background.

I ducked instinctually, the baseball bat missing me by inches as it sliced the air over my head. I turned towards him, but he was already on me, bringing the bat back around for another swing.

I managed to block the blow with my shotgun, the bat slamming into it, and knocking it out of my hands. *Fuck.*

I had just enough time to regret the costly error I'd made before Ryan tackled me to the ground, the full weight of his body slamming into mine. He pinned me, using the bat again to hold me down.

His face was distorted now, in anger and malice. The once familiar features painted with pure hatred, now there was no longer a need to hide behind a mask of mild contempt.

"It's not about killing you," he sneered, "it's about becoming you."

"Yeah, I got that part," I managed to breathe out as I struggled against him. I tried to peer around him, straining for a glimpse of Evelyn. She'd promised me she would stay in the little station. Assuming none of them could get inside, she should be safe enough.

But I didn't trust her to stay put. Keeping him talking, distracting him, wasn't the worst strategy for the moment. So long as she was still safe.

"Not just your bodies..." he continued, trailing off for a moment as he gripped me tightly by the chin, stilling me, the palm of his hand pressed over my windpipe. "You. Everything about you. Your lives." I froze, listening fully now. "So yes, Teddy. I was going to let you walk out of here, if none of them managed to claim you. That was the plan. And I would have walked out with you. As Ryan."

My eyes widened at his words, a wave of fear and dread running over my entire body, blood turning to ice in my veins as he continued. He was grinning down at me. "You're starting to understand now. Starting to get the picture."

I swallowed thickly, throat bobbing, pushing against his hand, as he continued to grip me, hand wrapped around my chin, holding that pressure on my neck. "The disappearances," I choked out. "All the people that disappeared out here. I read about them."

He nodded, with a snorting laugh. "And how many disappearances did you read about, Teddy? Hmm?" My mind raced to catch up, thinking. *Five... maybe six?* He seemed to be waiting for a response.

"A handful," I managed to grunt, my voice coming out strained. He was nodding at my words.

"That's right. Only a handful. Because those are the ones that failed." His grin widened, corners of his mouth stretching. "Those were the messy ones. The ones we learned from. But there have been more, Teddy. There have been so many more." His voice dropped to a whisper, and he leaned in closer to me, breath hot on my face. "Those are the ones you've never heard about. The ones where the person who walked into the woods... well, they walked back out again. Only they were different. Changed."

My heart was in my throat now. Tears of fear gathered unbidden, stinging in my eyes. He laughed, with Ryan's voice. A laugh that bubbled up from an endless well of cruelty. "That's right, boy. It was never the plan to just kill you. The plan was to take you. One by one. Replace you. Seamlessly, if possible." He shrugged, "I was willing to help them claim the rest of you. But no, I wasn't willing to blow my chance. Give up my spot." He shook his head, sighing. "And maybe, just maybe, you would have escaped. Made it out. I would have let you live, you know. If you had. I would have gone back as Ryan, nobody the wiser. And you could have gone on your way." He smiled again, a wicked smirk. "What a shame."

The howling came. Mournful, hungry cries. They were coming for me. Coming to claim me.

I thought then about dad. About how we had never seen him. And I thought about mom. Back at home. Thought of her opening the door, seeing him standing there on the porch. She'd have to invite him in, but once she did... "No," I gasped, stomach sick with dread. "No. Get the *fuck* off me," I growled. I moved my left hand, sliding it under my back, going for the handgun that pressed against my spine.

The thing masquerading as Ryan released his death grip on my chin, grabbing at my arm, pressing it against the ground, he tried to slide it in the opposite direction. I struggled against him, fighting back for every centimeter, muscles straining, reaching, fingers outstretched.

The howling continued, closer now. I could hear Evelyn screaming. The crack of her rifle. The whine as a bullet flew over Ryan's head. She must be too scared of hitting me, to risk shooting him in the back. That or she missed.

Ryan laughed, veins in his forehead standing out as he gained ground, shoving my arm farther away. "Fuck you, you piece of shit," I sputtered in his face, teeth clenched with the effort of straining against him.

I heard a barking yip off to my right. They were nearly here.

I leaned closer, until his eyes locked onto mine. "Go to hell," I murmured, as I slid the knife in my right hand up, and into his chest.

His eyes widened in shock, then his face crumpled. I felt his grip relax on my arm, and I managed to push up onto my left elbow, leaning forward, and pulling the knife, still in his chest, upwards, as I went, sliding it between his ribs.

I scrambled backwards, heels digging into the frozen earth, as I slid out from under him. I pulled the knife from his chest, and tipped him, until he was lying on his back. He was gasping and sputtering now. Red bleeding out onto the white snow and dirt beneath us, flecks of blood spraying from his open lips. I leaned forward, meaning to slit his throat, but I couldn't bring myself to do it.

I staggered back, moving away from him, and back towards Evelyn, scooping up my shotgun as I went. He was incapacitated enough, at the moment.

Evelyn was already running towards me. She threw her arms around me, pulling me close. I hugged her one armed, careful to keep the bloody knife off of her. "I'm okay," I murmured against her hair. "I'm alright."

She pulled away from me, tears in her eyes. "I thought I might hit you..." she started. "I was too scared to try. I'm sorry, Teddy. Thank God you're okay."

I nodded. "It's alright Ev. But we need to go. Now." I looked back at the woods behind us, expecting to see a pack of pale, white wolves bursting through the trees. "I think we should probably run, for a bit."

We couldn't risk hunkering down in the ranger's station. We'd be trapped in there. All they'd have to do was wait outside. Wait us out.

Evelyn nodded, slipping the strap of her rifle over her head. I did the same, slinging my shotgun over my back. I leaned down and wiped the knife in the snow, wiping the blade against the edge of the sole of my boot, before shoving it back into my pocket. Evelyn paused only once, for a few seconds, staring down at Ryan's body. Then she leaned over and picked up the wooden baseball bat, a grim expression on her face. She looked up at me and nodded. And then we ran.

22

— · —

We ran until we were out of breath. Legs pumping, lungs burning. Until the howling faded into the distance once again.

I used the time we spent catching our breath to pull out the map. Of course, I had no idea where we were exactly, but I eyeballed the area between trail #326 and Mount Snow and estimated it to be only another two to three miles from our rough position.

"We're so close," I gasped, turning to Evelyn as I refolded the map. She only nodded, still panting. The snow fell steadily still, each panting breath an escaping cloud in the air.

"Good," she managed after a moment. "I don't know how much more of this I can take." The sentiment hit me hard. Lack of sleep, adrenaline, surge after surge and then the crash. The cold. The fear, and anxiety. The grief. I was wearing thin, too. Worst of all (well, almost), my toes were frozen. I could feel it again now that we'd stopped. God I was sick of this. Sick of being cold. Sick of running. Sick of being scared. Of being hunted.

I nodded grimly back at her. "I know. But we're going to get out of here. We're so close," I repeated.

She blinked rapidly, trying to clear her eyes. She looked up at the sky, the snowflakes falling relentlessly down on her upturned face, and let out a deep breath.

"Ev." I moved closer to her, taking her half-frozen hand in mine. "It's going to be okay."

More tears threatened to spill. She shook her head, looking away from me. "Teddy..." she took a gasping breath. "It's already not okay."

"I know," I said, gut tight now with anger. Rage. Rage because I couldn't save them. Rage at the hopelessness of it all. "I know," I repeated. "But I won't let anything happen to you. I won't–"

Evelyn shook her head, cutting me off. "Teddy–"

"I won't, Ev." I slid my hand over her cheek, leaned my forehead against hers. "I promise you. I'll do anything I can. Everything I can. To make sure we walk out of here, together. Ourselves."

She let out a sob, nodding, eyelashes and cheeks damp. I kissed her on the forehead and pulled away from her. Wasting time. Time we didn't have.

"Come on," I said gently. "We need to keep moving. We're fighting against the daylight." I looked over at the horizon. "I'd say we have another hour, hour and a half, until we make it to Mount Snow." I swallowed, turning back to her. "It gets dark so early here; I think it'll be dusk, close to sunset, by the time we make it there."

Evelyn nodded, wiping her face with her gloved hands. "Okay," she said. "Maybe there will be people there. A crowd. Maybe we'll be safe."

I nodded back. "I hope so." I shrugged, "If not, we can take a shortcut through the woods, to get to the rental house. I don't know the exact route, but... I think I can get us to the right road; ballpark at least." I thought for a moment.

"If we can't find the house easily, we start knocking on doors. Any house we come across, until we find someone who can help us," Evelyn said, her voice gaining confidence. Steadying.

We started walking again. "Yeah..." I trailed off for a moment. "So, we'll have to be careful with who we trust." I sighed. I realized I hadn't filled her in yet about what Ryan had said to me at the end.

She stared at me, wide-eyed, listening as we walked. She was quiet for a long time afterwards. "Jesus Teddy," she said finally, eyes on her feet. She looked up at me. "How will we ever know we're safe?" She raised an eyebrow. "How many of them are... are out there... pretending to be... one of us?"

I shook my head, chest heavy with dread. I thought back to Ryan's earlier comment, when he was being snarky about us saying we'd been tracked into the woods. He'd said something about a random guy at the gas station in Burlington being off. I thought he'd been joking, just being an asshole, at the time. But the comment hit me differently now. Was that possible then? Could they really just be... anywhere? I glanced sideways at Evelyn; she watched me closely. "I don't know, Ev," I said quietly. "I really don't know."

23

— · —

We were making good time, but I could feel myself becoming more and more anxious as we went. The forest remained quiet around us, and we moved at a steady pace. I kept one eye on the sun's path, turning to check its position in the sky so often I was putting a crank in my neck.

We came upon a little campsite suddenly. A pair of tents, green canvas flapping in the wind, sat across from each other, a campfire in between.

The fire was still going. Logs burnt down until they were white hot, black and white ashes falling to the ground beneath the flames.

Evelyn and I turned to each other, eyes meeting. Her expression was guarded and cautious, but curious. "Hello?" she called out tentatively. "Is anyone here?"

My gut twisted, remembering the last time we'd run into strangers. I lifted the shotgun, not in position, but ready. I angled to the side, around a large wood pile, trying to get a view inside the far tent.

There was a lot of wood, I realized. A lot. Far more than anyone would be likely to gather for a night or two camping. And who went camping in the middle of November, anyway? It struck me as a little odd.

I felt my anxiety growing as I moved around behind the tent next to me, eyes on the dim interior of the far tent. I couldn't make out anyone inside. Some rumpled sleeping bags. A backpack. It looked like it was empty. I motioned to Evelyn to stay where she was. She gripped her rifle in one hand. Baseball bat in the other.

I moved swiftly around the closer tent. The flaps were down, but they weren't zipped. I reached out a hand and flung the closest flap back.

It was empty too. But there was blood. So much blood. All over the sleeping bags, kicked and twisted on the ground. *Fuck.*

I took a step back, retreating from the tent. I found Evelyn, and shook my head, expression grim. "There's no one here." I glanced at the woods around us. "There's blood," I said simply, nodding at the tent. "I think we should go."

Her eyes widened, but she nodded and moved around the tent to join me. We continued, moving past an upright log, an axe buried in the top. I heard something behind me and turned swiftly.

It was just Evelyn; she had one boot propped up on the log. She pumped the axe handle back and forth, until it dislodged from the stump. She'd set the baseball bat down on the ground.

"I think this'll be a bit more effective. Don't you?" she asked, grinning a little at my expression. She shrugged, and we moved on, falling in next to each other.

We didn't make it far until we came across the first one. I don't know what to call them. They were new– fresh, I guess. Recently changed.

We moved through a copse of pine, rows of brown knotted trunks, crowned in green swaying boughs. It was a woman. She was crouched down in a depression in the ground between two large pines.

She was naked. Bare skin practically glowing in the shadows beneath the pines. The ground was covered with needles beneath her. She was untouched by snow, the trees here growing so thick they offered some protection from the elements. She crouched over her knees, body bowed, head hanging down. Her black hair hung, long and limp, shielding her face.

We froze, about forty yards away. Evelyn looked up at me, eyes wide, a pleading look, a mix of fear and anguish. "What the hell is she doing?" I said, looking back and forth between Ev and the woman, scared to take my eyes off of her for too long. "It looks like she's..." I trailed off.

"In pain," Evelyn finished for me. She was staring at the woman now. Expression thoughtful. "She looks like she's in pain."

I studied her, not daring to take another step forward. "Do you think she's..." I shrugged. "Still human?" Evelyn looked up at me, brows wrinkled. I shrugged again. "I mean, we never found any bodies, did we?" Evelyn looked back over at the woman as I spoke.

"We still don't really know how this all works. Do they... possess us somehow? Take over our bodies? Or are they skinning us? Using our skins to turn into us? If so..." I shook my head. "We found that pot, with the arms and–"

Evelyn cut me off with a wave of her hand, shaking her head, "I haven't forgotten."

"Yeah. But no bodies..." I sighed. "I still don't think we have the full picture."

Evelyn's head cocked to the side, watching the woman, she took a step forward, off to the side, angling around her. She didn't seem to have noticed us at all. Didn't seem aware of our presence. "I dunno..." She shook her head after a moment. "I guess you're right. We don't really know how this all works." She studied the woman a moment longer. "But either way, I don't think so. I don't think she's still human, I mean." She shook her head again. "What do we do?" she whispered to me now, the axe gripped tightly in her hand.

"Well..." I trailed off again, uncertain. "I don't think we can just leave her..."

Evelyn shook her head, bending forward, hands on her knees, trying to peer at the woman's face. "I know. But..." She thought for a moment. "But I don't know if it's right. I don't know if it's right to... to..."

I nodded, licking my lips. The heavy feeling, the weight of dread in my chest was growing heavier by the moment. It was surrounding me now. Pressing down on my shoulders. The weight of sorrow. The weight of grief. The weight of knowing what needed to be done. And knowing there was no one else. No one else but me, to do it.

I felt so alone, suddenly, at that moment. I don't know why. But it was like it hadn't really sunk in, that my dad was gone. Dead. The full reality of that hadn't sunk in. Not until I stood there, under those trees. Watching that woman, that creature, suffering, realizing there would be no one to swoop in to help. No one to make the decision for me. I would have to figure it out myself. I don't think I've ever felt so alone in my life. I felt Evelyn's hand in mine, squeezing it. I looked down at her. And I don't know what I looked like at that moment. I can only imagine.

I blinked the tears out of my eyes and nodded, looking away, down at the ground. Down at my feet.

"It's okay, Teddy. Let's just leave. Let's just keep going. We'll go around her." She looked over at her. "I don't think she knows we're here anyway."

I looked up at the woman's bowed figure. Shaking now in minute convulsions. I really wanted to. I really wanted to do exactly what she was suggesting. But I shook my head no. "We can't risk it, Evelyn. We know nothing about them. These things." I nodded towards her. "We don't know how they work. Maybe it takes minutes. Maybe hours. Maybe she'll be after us before we know it. Maybe they can scent us. Clearly, they're tracking us somehow." I shook my head. "No. We need to take care of it."

Evelyn shook her head, hand falling out of mine. "I can't, Teddy." She looked up at me with wide eyes. "I don't think I can stand it. Not when she's like that." She gestured at her.

I swallowed. "Close your eyes, Evelyn. Turn around." She shook her head, lips quivering. "It'll be quick."

She turned slowly, turned her back on the woman, not meeting my eyes. Until she was facing the other way. She tucked the axe between her thighs, and lifted both hands up over her face, covering her eyes. Like she was counting for hide and seek. Like when we were little kids.

I took a deep breath, steeling myself. *Don't think. Just do it. Don't think.* She's not a person. Whoever she was, she's gone now. And this thing killed her. *This thing killed her.*

I moved forward now, my feet propelling themselves, my body moving on its own, taking over because my mind couldn't. Pine needles crunched beneath my boots. Even puffs of white, exiting with each breath into the air. I raised my shotgun, flicking off the safety, moving closer. Slowly closer.

And I waited. I waited for her to look up. To hear me. To respond in some way. And I watched. Watched myself moving closer to her. Watched her, oblivious, as she convulsed harder now.

The bones in her shoulder blades were sticking out, trailed by knobs of spine down her pale back. She must have been thin. Too thin. She moved. Her arms stretched out behind her, over her back. Reaching. Then sliding forward, sliding along the ground. There was something sinuous, animalistic, in her movements. She tipped her head back suddenly, as I moved closer, her dark hair a curtain, falling over her shoulders.

She eyed me. No surprise. No shock. Just coal dark eyes, framed with thick lashes. Her cupid's bow lips parted in a slow smile. The muscles around her mouth had that odd, unpracticed look. Rusty.

I aimed for her forehead. She let out a low, rough chuckle. Her voice was deep. Too deep, for that thin face, that small frame. And I realized with shock, taking in her tiny breasts, her narrow waist, that she probably wasn't a woman at all. A girl. A teenager. Maybe my age. Probably younger. Maybe even younger than Katie.

My finger froze mid-way, as it contracted over the trigger. Her grin widened, stretching until it looked impossibly big, her cheeks pinched, two balls of red.

"Put it down," she murmured, her voice still unnaturally deep, but sounding a little more real. A little more human. She cleared her throat. "Put the gun down." She cocked her head to the side. "I'm not going to hurt you." Her weight shifted back onto her ankles. "I pinky promise." Her voice was already smoother, higher. More feminine now. I felt a chill go down my back as the hair on my arms and neck stood on end. *Pinky promise.* Had this thing heard her say that? This poor girl, before it killed her? Had it watched her, peering out from the shadows, between branches. Stalked her, until it knew her voice. Her mannerisms. Until it could copy her.

I felt a surge of anger, that familiar rage, boiling suddenly in my gut. I recentered on her forehead, finger curling again over the trigger, as she shifted her weight back further and sprung.

I didn't know when their speed would stop taking me by surprise. Maybe never. But she moved impossibly fast. And she wasn't aiming for me.

She leapt up into the trees above. The round I'd shot whining uselessly beneath her feet. She'd managed to jump onto a branch up over my head. I darted forward, spinning as I went. She swung down on one arm, feet kicking out as I moved under her; she kicked me full force in the back, striking me with both feet.

I pitched forward, catching myself with both hands on the ground below, nails sliding into the dirt. I just managed to keep my face out of the pine needles. I felt one of my hearing aids pitch forward, hanging off my ear. The earmold thankfully hadn't been dislodged. My shot gun was underneath me; I'd landed half on it. My stomach aching dully where the metal had shoved into my gut. I thought of the knife in my pocket briefly, a flash of gratitude that it hadn't somehow stuck me in the gut. Imagine dying on my own knife, after all of this. I reached behind my back and grabbed the handgun, rolling over just as she landed over me.

She crouched over me, one hand sliding forward, down my chest, as she smiled wickedly at me. She opened her mouth to speak, and I brought the handgun up between us, and shot her in the chest. Not quite hitting her in the heart, but close enough.

Her body jerked backwards, then tipped forward, a shocked expression on her face. A thin trickle of blood ran down, from the corner of her lips. I squeezed the trigger again, aiming between her eyes. Her head snapped back, and she landed on top of me in a heap, a gurgling sound coming from her throat. I shoved her off of me in disgust, scrambling to the side. More blood. More blood all over my coat.

I had the sudden image of Evelyn and I, finally stumbling out of the woods, surrounded by cop cars, lights flashing. My hands raised. Coated in blood. How would I ever explain that I hadn't actually killed anyone? Hadn't hurt anyone. Not really.

I shoved back with the heels of my boots. Reaching up to slide my hearing aid back behind my ear when I was sure she was no longer moving.

Evelyn had turned around again. She was facing me, eyes wide, hands covering her mouth.

She ran over to me, while I managed to get to my feet on shaky legs. I pulled several bullets out of my pocket and reloaded the handgun. Flicking the safety back on and shoving it back in my belt. She made it to me, hands patting on my chest, then my face. Wiping off the smear of blood she'd transfer to my cheek. "Are you okay? Are you hurt?"

I shook my head. "No," I gasped, realizing I was panting. "I'm not. I'm not hurt, I mean." I shook my head again, looking down at her too small body, sprawled on the ground, and chuckled slightly. "Although, to be clear, I'm not okay, either," I panted. "Let's go. We need to get the fuck out of these woods." I shook my head, moving over to pick up my shotgun. "I'm never going hunting again."

Evelyn grinned a little. Licking her lips, she said, "Yeah, me either. To be clear, I'm never stepping foot in the fucking woods again. For any reason." I chuckled back, as she looked from the body on the ground, over to me. "And I'm not leaving you alone like that again. To face one of them." She nodded down at the body. "We stick together." She looked back at me. "Deal?"

I looked her in the eyes, those green pools I wanted to drown in, wanted to know. Every fleck, every speckle of gold– I wanted to know them all. Memorize every one. I nodded slowly. "Deal."

24

— · —

We came across two more, in rapid succession. Both naked, just like the first. Clearly in a state of transition. Transformation. But after our experience with the first, there wasn't the same reluctance, the same hesitation.

The next was a man, dark hair cut short. Probably the girl's dad, I thought with a twinge of grief. I used the handgun.

He was draped over what looked like a dead tree. Chest wedged between the branches, one arm hanging down, stretching. His body twitched, head lolling then jerking back. Like a corpse slowly coming back to life. Reanimating. I didn't give him a chance to gain consciousness.

The next was a woman. Long, thick, blonde hair, falling in loose waves. She was leaning against a large tree, on the far side. I almost didn't see her. Wouldn't have, if it hadn't been for her hair, it stood out in a landscape of browns and greens. She was further along, by the time we got to her. Her hands were wrapped around the trunk of the tree. She moved sinuously, like the others. Hands running over the bark like it was fine velvet, caressing it, almost. I wanted to look away. I didn't want to watch. Didn't want to see her face, with its ghoulish expression and too-wide smile.

Her skin was white like porcelain. She peeked at me from behind the tree. The fingers on one hand curling, beckoning me closer. My gut twisted as I aimed, taking her down. I didn't breathe again until she was still.

Evelyn was true to her word. She stayed with me, for them both. Refused to leave my side or look away. She grimaced at me after the last one, an odd expression of revulsion and curiosity on her face, as she eyed the woman's naked body lying in the snow.

We moved faster then. I didn't want to risk coming on another one of them too quickly, but at the same time, they seemed to be moving more slowly as they woke up, for lack of a better term. I reasoned it may be better to come upon them sooner rather than later, and we picked up our pace, cold, sore feet screaming in protest.

I'd been distracted, too busy scanning the surrounding woods to pay attention to the sun. I took in the quality of light suddenly and glanced behind us to see the sun moving behind grey clouds, hovering closer to the horizon. It would be dusk soon. Another reason to move faster.

The terrain was more level here, flatter than it had been back in the Glastenbury Wilderness. Less hills, less rocky outcrops. I was grateful for that, if nothing else. It meant the last leg of our journey should go faster.

But I could feel that sense of dread sinking in, digging its talons into my heart as it filled my chest. The light seemed to be fading faster and faster now, and I felt a new urgency; we were running out of time.

The light around us had taken on an ethereal quality now. The murky dusk deepened the shadows beneath the trees. The woods took on that hushed feeling just before night falls, as though the entire forest was holding its breath, waiting for what was about to come.

Evelyn and I eyed each other as we neared the clearing. I realized it wasn't just a clearing, but a break in the trees. The trees were more sparse here, growing less thick.

"We're close now," I murmured to her. "I think Mount Snow is just up ahead." And I could see it as I spoke; the peak just visible rising behind the gentle hill ahead of us. The trees were thicker again on the hill. Maybe just one more hill, one more grove, and we'd be out. I felt a flood of relief. Of emotion. *You get them out. You get yourself out.*

"Let's go." Evelyn nodded, her lips stretching in a hesitant smile.

25

— • —

We made quick work of cresting the hill, moving silently and swiftly between the trees. I eyed the shadows we passed with a flash of apprehension, but I didn't slow. We were too close now. Too close to let anything stop us. To let anything slow us down. Mount Snow loomed in front of us, the ski runs visible, crisscrossing the mountain face.

I felt tears prickle in the corner of my eyes. *But we aren't safe yet,* I told myself. We needed to stay focused. Not let our guard down for even a minute.

We moved swiftly down the hill, and I could feel myself bursting with renewed energy; we were going to make it.

It was nearly dark, as we reached the base of the mountain. A large building stood up ahead, visible through the trees, past an empty parking lot.

I felt my chest deflate a little at the sight. Not a single car was parked in the lot. Evelyn and I eyed each other for a moment, agreeing wordlessly to keep going.

Maybe there was someone, a worker, here after hours, parked in the back. Maybe there would be someone still here, closing up for the night.

We moved through the parking lot, the sound and feel of my feet crunching through the snow onto pavement one of the most oddly beautiful things I'd ever experienced. Back in civilization. Out of the woods. *Thank fucking god.*

We moved swiftly through the thin row of trees separating the parking lot and the lodge at the base of the mountain.

I eyed the sprawling building wearily. There were no lights on inside, the windows pitch black squares in a blank facade. Evelyn sighed loudly next to me, shoulders slumping forward.

"Well, I guess that was too much to hope for." She shrugged at me. "What do we do now? Do we try to break in?"

I eyed the set of double doors to our right. I was sure we could figure out a way. We had the axe. Worse case we could break a window and climb through. I paused, thinking. "I really don't know what we should do, Ev." I turned to her. "We could break a window, even if we can't get through the doors. Those look pretty solid, at least." There were no windows in the thick-looking doors. "If we break in, climb through a window, there could be a burglar alarm triggered. That might call the police out here automatically, even if we can't find a phone in there," I said slowly, "which I'm sure there must be one."

Evelyn eyed the nearest window, nodding slowly. She turned to look at me, eyes sweeping up and down my body. "Even if you take your coat off, you're still covered in blood," she said quietly. "It's all over your shirt too. At least at the collar."

I looked down at my shirt, tucking my chin into my neck. She was right, unfortunately. Blood soaked the front of my shirt. "Fuck," I said glumly, eyeing the doors. "I'm going to look like an axe murder," I mumbled.

Evelyn giggled a little, "And I have the axe," she said, holding it aloft.

I grinned at her. "So, what do we do?" I said after a moment. I eyed the trail that led around the building. "Do we head for the house?" I looked up at the sky, at the streetlamps sprinkled down the trail, casting the ground below in a golden glow. "It's practically dark now, but it's not that much further."

It leapt off the roof, and time slowed down, lagging, as it appeared to hang there, suspended in the air for a horribly long, sickening moment. Its limbs were grotesquely long. Pale, muscled arms splayed, ending in hands with long sharp claws. Powerful legs bending at the knees as it sprung. And it's face... The face was all mouth. A wide black maw, lined with long, thin teeth, top and bottom, like sharp slivers of bone. Its eye sockets were large and sunken in; the only sign of an orb within was the glint of reflected light off the center, as it fell.

I heard Evelyn's scream, echoing through the empty grounds. Faintly. As though it was coming from far away. It landed on its feet in front of the double doors, in the center of the path, crouching low, down on all fours. Claws curled into the snow-covered gravel.

We ran. We sprinted down the trail, below the streetlamps. I could hear the howling now, faintly rising in the distance, coming from the woods, in the direction of the hill we'd crossed only minutes before.

I gripped my shotgun in one hand, strap still strung around me, to stop it from bouncing as I ran. I debated stopping, turning to aim, but it would take too long. I couldn't be sure I could pull it off before it was on us. It was too fast. Thank God we'd had a lead to start; it had landed maybe 50 yards away from us.

I reached for the handgun, hand sliding below my coat. *Please don't drop it. Don't drop it.* I felt my fingers on the rough cross-hatching on the grip and managed to slide my hand around it and pull it loose. I ran with it in my left hand for several steps, flicking off the safety as I went. I could hear the monster behind us. Gaining on us.

I felt the hot flame of fear spreading through my gut, up my chest, threatening to overwhelm me. The panic. The unrelenting fear that gripped and squeezed, and wouldn't let go, threatening to consume me. I shoved it down. Down deep. And I leaned forward, head bowing as we ran. Evelyn's footsteps on the gravel beside me. I felt my eyes narrow, my breathing still. *You can do this.* I whispered to myself. And I turned.

Arm coming up in an arc, my left hand sliding under the butt of the grip, right hand melding over the trigger. I aimed as instinct took over, and I squeezed the trigger. Hitting it in the eyes. Those dark holes of black.

I squeezed off two shots, rapidly. Then aimed at its chest for good measure as it began to stumble, long limbs folding over each other. It let out a keening howl, chilling my bones, as it crumpled into a heap and slid several feet across the gravel path.

I looked back, behind it. Evelyn had slowed and come to a stop behind me. There were more. So many more, howling off in the distance. I reloaded the handgun, fingers moving steadily, but not fast enough. Nowhere near fast enough.

"Teddy," Evelyn breathed behind me. "Which way?" She held her hands out, axe still gripped in her right hand, gesturing to the trees up ahead. "Do we go through the trees, or follow the road?" I eyed the trail; it curved through scattered trees and exited into what looked like another parking lot, and the road beyond.

"Fuck!" I yelled, "I dunno!" I felt the panic rising again. "I dunno... I guess the woods? That should be shorter. So it should be faster, right? Cut through the trees!"

We turned and ran, veering off the well-lit path, heading for the darkness of the woods. I paused at the treeline, one hand on Evelyn's arm, turning back at the sound of scrambling behind us, gravel shifting.

Another of the creatures was sprinting down the path on all fours, running like some sort of bone-white, skin-covered, demonic horse, slobber dripping from its open gaping maw. I handed Ev the handgun, slapping it down into her open palm. I lifted my shotgun this time, sighting in the thing's grotesque face, shooting it right between the eyes.

We didn't wait to watch it die, we turned and started running. Running through the trees once more.

26

—•—

I led Evelyn on in what I hoped was a straight shot, weaving through the thick trees. My brain raced, trying to recall the memory of this section of the map. There was no time to stop to check.

I knew the street with the rental houses lay on the other side of the ski lodge on the map. I was sure it wasn't the first street past the mountain, but I thought it branched off of that.

We were basically sprinting now, moving as fast as we could given the trees, and the branches and terrain. I could hear howling still in the distance, moving steadily closer to our position. What I didn't know was the scale we were looking at. This patch of wood had looked miniscule on the map, but how far was it exactly, until we would come out on the other side?

We just had to make it to the house, I told myself. Make it to the house, and they wouldn't be able to come inside. Well, none of them except for Ryan, I thought with a jolt.

It may have only been five minutes, but it felt like it took ages for us to cross that strip of wood. I breathed a little easier as we burst through the trees on the other side. We found ourselves on the side of a road. It stretched into darkness before us in either direction.

"Which way?" Evelyn gasped, her voice half a sob. "Right?" She looked over at me, the whites of her eyes visible.

I nodded at her in the dark. "Yeah, right. Then I think we should come to a sharp left," I panted, "and we should be on our street."

She nodded, and we took off once again, footsteps crunching through the snow as we ran out in the middle of the road.

There had clearly been at least one car that passed through here not too long ago; there were tire ruts in the snow. But they weren't super recent; a fresh layer of snow had fallen since then.

Evelyn whipped her head around, steps faltering, and I turned back, peering over my shoulder. I could hear it now too; the sound of breaking branches, just as one of them burst through the trees down the road behind us.

I stopped immediately, lifting my shotgun once more, attempting to sight it in. It was getting harder now, as the darkness swiftly grew deeper around us with each passing minute. I was thankful they were so pale, almost white, allowing it to stand out against the background of the dark woods. I aimed at its chest, not trusting myself to hit it in the head from this distance in the dark.

I thought I saw it jerk, and figured the round had hit home. I heard a shriek next to me, and turned to see Evelyn, axe lifted behind her back. She whipped it forward, and it left her hand, spinning twice, smacking right into the face of a second skin-walker with a sickening thud. It had loomed out of nowhere from the treeline directly next to us.

I swiftly shot it in the chest as it stilled, swaying back and forth for a few seconds.

"Jesus Ev, good throw," I breathed at her, eyebrows raised, and she looked at me, and shrugged, the ghost of a smile on her lips made my gut tighten.

She moved over to the creature, gripped the handle, and pulled it loose. The end of the axe dribbled blood onto the snow below.

"Let's go," I panted. And we continued on, sprinting down the street, until we came to a juncture, and I saw with a flood of relief, the road split, branching off to the left, in a sharp turn.

We took the corner at a sprint, my boots sliding a little as we rounded the curve. We ran as hard as we could. I realized Evelyn was starting to fall behind me a bit. I slowed my pace, turned and ran backwards a few paces, eying the road behind us, and the dark treeline off to our right. I realized they would be more likely to break through the trees to the right then follow us around the corner and down the road.

"House!" Evelyn gasped, pointing behind me. I spun in the direction she pointed, eyeing the house as we moved closer. "That's not it," she gasped, calling out to me. "Must be Dr. C's." The driveway was empty, and the lights were off. It didn't look like anyone was there.

"Next one," I gasped, calling back. A quarter of a mile, I remembered. Ryan had said it couldn't be more than a quarter of a mile down the road.

I strained, listening for howling in the distance. But it seemed to be quiet now. Only the wind and our footsteps were audible to me.

I spied the end of a driveway a few minutes later and felt a flood of relief washing over me. This had to be it.

I pointed at the end of the driveway, and we made our way towards it. A light flooded on, momentarily stunning me, as we reached the driveway.

It was the motion-sensored light over the garage. Dr. Carter's black Lincoln sat parked out front, covered in snow. Evelyn let out a sob next to me, and we scrambled for the porch.

I paused on the driveway, watching our backs as she moved to the porch, I scanned the road, but saw nothing. No pale figures sprinting towards us. I turned and followed her. Our feet slamming up the steps, onto the porch. The door handle opened easily in her grasp, and she turned to me with tears in her eyes as she shoved it open, and we tumbled inside.

I turned to face the door as Evelyn slammed it shut behind us.

27

—•—

I breathed a sigh of relief, the air rushing out of my chest. My shoulders slumped forward. Evelyn turned to face me, slamming her back against the door, chest heaving.

I froze as her eyes went wide. She stared behind me, over my left shoulder.

I turned, jumping back, and moved to her side at the door. I gaped over at the family room, my stomach sinking. Blood. Splattered all over the couch. The funky 80s pattern stained pink and red. More blood trailed from the couch over towards the French glass doors.

I turned to Evelyn as she bent forward, hands clasped together, gripping the axe handle in front of her stomach. She gasped in silent sobs. I slid an arm around her shoulders, bringing my finger to my lips, urging her to stay quiet. She sobbed harder, screaming noiselessly, tears streaming down her face as she doubled over. I caught her, wrapping my other arm around her, I pulled her to me. She pressed her face against my chest, heaving deep gasping sobs, one hand gripping my coat.

I held her, squeezing her to me as she shook with grief. I moved her after a moment, pulling her gently with me as I headed into the kitchen, entering the room first, and scanning it quickly, confirming it was empty.

I moved over to the window and peered out. But I could see nothing. The motion sensor light we had tripped on the way in must have turned back off again. I was greeted by a pitch-black night. The front yard was an expanse of white; no pale creatures stalked towards the house.

I moved us back over to the front door, and knelt down, pulling Evelyn gently down with me. I put my lips right next to her ear. "We need to look for the keys, Ev," I whispered. "The keys to Dr. Carter's car. It's still out front."

Evelyn shook her head, trying to calm her tears. She grasped my face, setting the axe down on the carpet. She turned my ear towards her mouth. "I saw him give the keys to Mrs. Sandy," she murmured. "She could still have them... on her." My gut clenched and I shook my head in desperation.

I turned back to face her. "No, we're going to find them, okay?" I murmured. "You start looking in the kitchen, okay?"

She nodded glumly and moved slowly to her feet, grabbing the axe again, she moved through the kitchen doorway, glancing back at me as she went.

I eyed the stairway leading to the lower level with suspicion, as I moved out into the middle of the room. I checked the little bathroom to the right of the front door as I went, verifying it was truly empty.

My gaze moved upwards, as I headed over to the dining table, catching and pausing on the half wall over my head. The loft. I was hit with a spike of horror. I saw the creature leaping off the roof of the lodge in my mind's eye and pictured its head appearing over that half wall of the loft. Pictured it landing on top of me. I kept my back to the outer wall of the house as I moved through the room, and my eyes on the loft.

I quickly swept over the table; covered in the random junk people had set down, but no car keys were visible. I pulled the handgun back out of my belt as I went, making sure the safety was off.

I moved swiftly over to the fireplace, eyes still on the loft, trying to keep my footsteps as quiet as possible. We had slammed the door shut, when we entered. It wasn't like we hadn't announced our presence already. But I didn't want to make it any easier for them to find me.

My gaze fell on Dad's cell phone and pager, still sitting on the mantel where he had left them. I grabbed his cell, shoving it in the front pocket of my coat along with the hunting knife. There was no signal out here, but maybe if we could find the car keys, get out to a main road, we could get a signal.

I scanned the rest of the mantel and the coffee table but found nothing there. I eyed the cryptids book with a stab of grief and moved swiftly back around the armchair. As I passed the French glass doors, I peered out into the backyard.

I jumped slightly, freezing for a moment. A dark figure stood there, in the middle of the little trail that led back to the clearing. Easily made out against the light background of snow behind him.

I knew instantly it was Dr. Carter. I could make out the silhouette of his hair. A glint of metal from his glasses. He stood stock still, almost like he was watching me through the window.

I felt a sick twist of fear, and I moved over towards the kitchen. I scooped up my backpack as I went. I would need a change of clothes. There was no time to get anything else. It was time to go. Who knew who could get into the house now. And who knew what was already inside with us.

I practically bumped into Evelyn as she exited the kitchen. She held up a hand, car keys dangling from her fingers. I grinned at her, nodding briefly, I grasped her hand in mine, covering the gently clinking car keys.

"Shh," I murmured. "We need to go, now. I just saw someone in the backyard. I think it's Dr. C. Let's go."

We turned and left. I pulled the door shut gently behind us, and we moved swiftly down to the car. Evelyn handed me the keys, and she moved over to the passenger side. I cursed the light flooding the driveway, announcing our location.

She pulled her coat sleeve down further over her hand, and gripping it, she started wiping snow off the windshield. I brushed the light covering of snow off the lock, and inserted the key, turning it and yanking the handle. I set the handgun down on the center console and tossed my backpack into the backseat.

I copied Evelyn, clearing snow from the driver's side windshield with my arm. She had moved to the rear of the car and was clearing off the back windshield. I eyed the darkness, the street behind her, gaze flickering back and forth as I watched for Dr. Carter to appear around the side of the house.

Evelyn finished and moved quickly to pull open the passenger door. She yanked on the handle and looked up at me. I realized it was still locked.

I leaned in and hit the button to unlock the car, and we both climbed in, car doors slamming loudly in the silence.

I inserted the key in the ignition. And it wasn't until that moment that it occurred to me that they might have disabled this car, too. I hadn't even thought about checking the tires.

I looked at Evelyn, my eyes locking onto hers, as I twisted the key. The engine roared to life immediately, and the radio kicked on, distorted music and static coming through the speakers, and a grin broke out on her face. Her cheeks and lashes were still damp with tears, but she nodded, grinning widely at me.

I couldn't help but grin back. I held down the brake and shifted the car into reverse. I checked the rearview mirror as I went, pulling out into the street.

I paused, braking in the middle of the empty road, shifting into drive. I hit the gas, and we shot forward, tires grinding the snow beneath us into the dirt road.

28

— · —

We drove in silence for several minutes. The snow appeared to fly towards us as we went, white puffs hurtling into and over the windshield.

I tried to recall street names and turns as we went. Evelyn opened the glove compartment, searching for a map, but she came up empty-handed.

We came eventually to what looked like a main road. It wasn't a dirt road, at least, which was promising. I caught a glimpse of streetlights, up ahead in the distance, and what looked like black pavement in the tire ruts in the snow. I decided to turn left, wanting to take us south, away from the mountain. Away from the woods.

Evelyn still held the axe, tucked in her lap. Her rifle was resting at her feet, leaning against the seat and the door. I had placed my shotgun on the other side of her, within arm's reach. The handgun lay on the console still.

I scanned the side of the road, eyes flickering over the edge of the woods as we drove.

We reached the first streetlight and passed beneath it. Streetlights were a very good sign we were heading in the right direction. I made another left turn at the next juncture, and we continued on our way.

As I drove, streetlights lining the road on either side in even intervals now, my eyes flickered up instinctively to the rearview mirror.

I stilled, eyeing the vehicle on the road behind us. It was several hundred yards back. I pulled the cell phone out of my pocket and handed it to Evelyn. "Here," I murmured to her. "Hopefully we can get back to civilization. I can get cleaned up, and change. And hopefully we can get a signal, and call..." Call who? I thought? My mom... I guess. "Call for help," I finished.

Evelyn nodded, lips a thin line, and she looked back out the passenger window, eyes trained on the woods flying by.

My eyes returned to the rearview mirror, and I watched the vehicle behind us now as I drove, keeping one eye on the mirror.

It looked like an SUV, I decided. And I slowed our pace a little, letting it gain on us a bit. We rounded a bend, road curving to the right. I straightened out the Lincoln, and I eyed the mirror again, just as the SUV took the curve, and passed below a streetlamp.

I could just make out from the angle, the broken passenger window; jagged shards of glass still hanging down. And it was grey. A grey SUV.

I swallowed, my throat suddenly dry. I obviously couldn't see the back of it. But I knew in my gut that if I could, it would be covered in bumper stickers. *'All you need is LOVE!'* I glanced sideways at Evelyn, but she seemed completely unaware that we were now being followed. I watched it in the mirror for another minute or two. But I was sure.

We were still out in the middle of nowhere; likely passing just south of the Glastenbury Wilderness now. The dirt road we'd taken in to park our cars yesterday morning probably joined directly up to this one. Had they been sitting there, waiting for us, just in case we tried to drive out? I pictured the grey SUV sitting with its headlights off at the end of the dirt road leading into the woods. A dark shadowy figure in the driver's seat; eyes on the road ahead, waiting for us. I cleared my throat, looking over at Evelyn.

"Ev," I started, "behind us, the SUV–"

"Teddy!" she squealed, legs pressing forward like she was slamming on an imaginary brake. I hit the brake myself, eyes whipping back to the road ahead.

One of the creatures burst into the middle of the road. It was big. The biggest one we'd seen. Huge. Its long limbs seemed to reach nearly to the streetlamp above as it ran, stretching and bending grotesquely as it moved. It was too late. And the road was too slick.

We slid, smashing into the thing; taking out its rear legs, and tipping it, tossing it over the car, a loud *thunk-thunk* as limbs ricocheted off the roof.

The car went into a spin, and I couldn't control it, panicking, as I tried braking harder, then I remembered to pump the brakes as the car continued to slide. We spun sideways, turning around to face in the opposite direction, as we finally slid to a stop. Evelyn's screaming died down for a moment and then she gasped and screamed again.

I barely had time to react. I felt myself moving too slow, as the creature's face appeared under the streetlight to our left, maw open in a feral howl of rage as it limped over to us, scrambling over the slick snow on twisted, damaged limbs.

I pulled the shotgun from the passenger footwell and flicked the safety off. But Evelyn was already grabbing her rifle. She opened her door, and stepping out of the car with one leg, leaned out and shot at the thing as it loped towards us, screaming with feral rage herself. I pushed my door open and joined her.

The creature teetered back and forth on weak legs, until it eventually slumped over onto its side, and moved no more.

Evelyn looked over at me, chest heaving, shaking her head. I swallowed and eyed the grey SUV. It had come to a stop in the lane, headlights shining on us, no movement visible.

I nodded towards it. "That's the grey SUV, from the woods," I said, looking over at her. Her eyebrows went up in surprise, and she eyed it warily. Then she looked back at me.

I pumped the shotgun. "I'll be right back, Ev." She studied me for a moment, her gaze flickering over my features.

"Okay, Teddy," she said, "but I'll be right behind you." She stepped out of the car, leaving the door open, and nodded to me.

I nodded back, and moved forward, feet crunching through the snow once more. As I approached the SUV, the driver's side door swung open, and a man climbed out.

I knew it would be him. Somehow, I just knew. He pulled his familiar shotgun through the door with him, and I watched as he held it aloft, the muzzle pointed in my direction but angled down at the road.

"Teddy," he called out to me. And his voice was so right. So familiar. So perfect, that it brought tears to my eyes instantly.

I just stared at him, blinking rapidly, trying to keep my vision clear.

"I got them out," I said, my voice cracking a little. "Just like you said." I shrugged after a moment. "Well, Evelyn, at least." I wiped a sleeve over my eyes.

"I'm proud of you, Teddy," he said, voice calm.

"Yeah?" I called back, half a chuckle, half a sob.

"Of course I am, son. I've always been proud of you." I knew it wasn't him. Couldn't possibly be him. But I felt a desperate surge of hope, of pathetic pride, at his words. His face was calm, his eyes trained on me. Could he have made it, somehow? Could he have managed to survive?

I swallowed thickly. Keeping my voice steady was a struggle. "Son?" I chuckled darkly. "Then what's my real name, Dad?"

"What?" he asked, brows lifted in confusion. "Your real name?"

"Yeah," I said, heart sinking. "You heard me. What's my real name if you're my dad? Or better yet," I continued, an edge of anger creeping into my voice now, "what's yours?" He just stared at me, shaking his head. I saw the end of his shotgun twitch, lift, almost imperceptibly. I felt a hot surge of rage and grief flooding through me. I took several stuttering steps towards him. "What's your *real* name, you son of a bitch? Huh?" I was yelling now. "Tell me your real name. Say it. So I can say it back. So you can die. And stay dead."

"Teddy... son," he sighed, "it doesn't have to be this way."

"Yes!" I cried, "it does." I held a palm out. "What–what are you even talking about? Do you think you could ever actually replace him, you sick fuck?" Tears were streaming down my face now, unbidden, and I couldn't stop them. "Let us go!" I screamed at him, my voice breaking. "Just let us go." I shook my head. "Don't follow us... just..." I felt myself breaking now. I was at the end of my strength. I stared at him, searching for any hint, any shred of humanity that might be left. I flashed back to my last conversation with Ryan; how he had said he would have walked out beside us.

"Look." I fought to keep my voice calm, reasonable. "You got what you wanted, didn't you? You got a... a body... You can go anywhere now. With *his* face. I won't try to stop you," I said, voice firm now. And I meant it. As hard as it would be, to think of him, out there somewhere, wearing my dad's face, I meant it. "But please," my voice dropped, almost to a whisper. "Please, just let us go."

He watched me solemnly for a moment. And I saw it, then. A flicker of indecision. Like he was actually considering it. And it made me pause. I wondered for the first time *who*, not just *what*, these creatures actually were. Had they truly been human once, like the stories claimed? Had they become monsters, having completed some terrible act? Maybe they were just trying to become human once again. Trying to get back what they lost. I felt an odd twist of grief, even pity, course through my gut, as I watched him.

The thing wearing my dad's face shook his head slowly. "I can't do that, son," he said quietly. "I'm sorry."

I lifted and aimed in one smooth movement, taking him by surprise. It was my only advantage. I was a faster shot than my dad had been. I prayed that would hold true; that he wouldn't have time to react.

The shot hit home, right between his eyes. He remained standing for a long beat, suspended frozen in the air. And then he fell. Body crumpling to the ground.

I let out a strangled sob, lowering the shotgun. I turned to check on Evelyn. She stood a few yards behind me; rifle still trained on the spot where he had stood.

I moved slowly towards him. Towards the grey SUV. And as I walked, the cone of light from the headlights stretched my shadow, until it looked impossibly tall; long limbs contorted and grotesque, moving oddly over the snow.

I lifted the shotgun and shot out the front tires. First the right one, then the left.

I leaned down when I reached him and nudged him with the end of the shotgun, suddenly scared that he was playing dead. That he would lunge for me, grab me by the ankles, and pull me down with him into hell.

But his body jiggled at my nudging and nothing more. I reached down, shaking slightly now, trembling from the cold. From the fear. From the adrenaline and grief.

He was wearing Dad's clothes. I reached into the right back pocket of his jeans, fingers wrapping around his wallet. I pulled out the familiar worn brown leather and running a thumb over it, I flipped it open. His driver's license was there; his familiar smiling face staring back at me, with our home address printed off to the side.

"I got out, Dad," I murmured. "I got us out." I slipped the wallet into my pocket and headed back to the car. Back to Evelyn.

We climbed in wordlessly, and I shifted the car into drive, slowly pulling it around to face in the right direction again.

We took off down the road. After a minute or two, Evelyn reached down and pulled off her gloves, and I felt her hand slip into mine. I looked over at her, and she smiled back at me, her lips curling in that familiar smile, her frizzy red curls wild from the wind. Her eyes were liquid green, flecks of gold sparkling under the streetlamp.

I faced the road ahead, but my eyes flickered periodically up to the rearview mirror, and to the empty road behind us.

THE END

About the Author

A.C. Hessenauer describes herself as an author of horror thrillers with gothic romance vibes. A.C. is an active member of the Horror Writers Association. When she's not participating in macabre ceremonies dedicated to the eldritch horrors out in the woods, A.C. enjoys spending time with her family; her husband, two sons, and border collie named Maximus. She loves a good horror movie, and of course, getting swallowed whole by a good book.

---•---

Also by

Dread House, 2024
Possession, 2024
Mount Snow, 2025
Carl: An Easter Horror Thriller Novella, 2025
Jumpers, 2025
MANIMAL, 2025

DREAD HOUSE PUBLISHING

Check out our website; Dread House Publishing, for news on upcoming releases, and to sign up for a monthly newsletter with ARC opportunities at www.dreadhousepublishing.com or scan the QR code below.

www.ingramcontent.com/pod-product-compliance
Lightning Source LLC
Chambersburg PA
CBHW060310260626
47160CB00007B/2555